WHAT A FOOTBALLER!

JOHN ROSE

PROLOGUE

One day, after a game, when the boys were arguing in loud voices how much each one had done during the match, a beggar walked up. We'd never seen him on that street. He couldn't have weighed much more than 100 pounds. A walking skeleton, possessed by the ghost of misery, a character in a wretched state, with a gloomy look and torn clothes. He looked like someone who'd been sleeping on the streets for a long time.

"Hey, kids," he said, "I really liked watching you play. Yup, really liked it a lot. A long time ago... I was a famous player. Scored goals. Everybody knew my name. I can still hear that name echoing today. Now I'm poor. I'm nothing. When you got everything, you're everything. When you got nothing, you're nothing."

The guys knew lots of other beggars. They were used to dealing with them, because hundreds of beggars wandered the streets prayed for bread, home and work. And the guys knew that old age and extreme poverty made people senile. But just to be mean and have some fun they decided to mock the old beggar.

One of them asked, "What was your name when you were a star?"

"I don't remember. My memory's fading," the old guy said, hanging his head. "But I scored goals, lots of goals!"

"Yeah, for sure," another kid shot back, smiling from ear to ear. "You still hear the echo of your name being screamed in every city. Just the echo!"

The old man kept on describing his past, with a melancholy air, always the same way, so that all the kids could recite his litany by memory. Feeling himself mocked by all those kids, the windbag claptrap ended up begging our pardon and asking to take his leave, and off he went, calmly, to hoots of laughter. Holding on to one another, laughing until they cried, the boys barely had the strength to lift up their hands and say goodbye to the old geezer.

The mockery had not yet faded when another old man came over, breathing heavily. He'd come out of his building, running down six flights of stairs, as soon as he recognized Goldstone, as he was walking off.

"So you guys don't know who he is? He's Goldstone! A legendary player! He scored more than 60 goals for the national team! A king of football! He had the world at his feet!"

The boys were in a state of shock once they knew the identity of the man they had just been mocking. So he had told the truth after all. He had been a star. A world-class star. He was known to all society, and deserved to be. One day his energy failed and forced him to stop, his money evaporated, and then the society that had applauded him turned its back on him.

Sad and contrite, the guys began to run after him, taking huge strides and knocking over garbage cans. Unfortunately, they could no longer catch sight of the idol they now sought to find. He had blended into the crowd of workers and beggars that crisscrossed the street leading downtown. And how they cried, repenting! A star had been there among them. He had not been a ghost. Or rather he had been a ghost.

On my street there was one open space: a warehouse without a roof, long since abandoned when its owners went bankrupt. This served as a football field for the kids, including me. We took the games seriously. There were tournaments for the teams, shoes for the players, leather balls, nets behind the goal, lines traced on the floor and a whistle for whoever acted as referee. A fast kind of football that we really fought over.

The backers of this little improvised club were the only successful men on the block that I grew up on: pimps, thieves and gangsters of the most varied calibers. They gave the players, like me, everything in abundance, in return for petty tasks that came up in the big city, like spying on people or carrying small packages or envelopes whose contents we knew nothing of.

I first began to kick a ball around when I was five years old. I was so short that I couldn't get the ball off the ground. Even if I jumped up as high as I could I didn't reach the shoulders of the boys who played defense on the opposing team. I wanted to be a striker and would not accept any other position. Sometimes, in special circumstances, I would agree to play defense or midfield, but I wouldn't stay there for long. As soon as the game began I would begin moving forward bit by bit until I was where I wanted to be.

My parents hated it that my legs and arms got scratched on the irregular floor of the old warehouse where we played. They thought that a skinny boy like me shouldn't even be there – without shin-guards, exposed to the pointed shoes of much bigger and more aggressive boys.

Many of those players in potentia really knew how to control the ball. They knew how to deaden its flight with their chest, hip or the tip of their shoe; but after that they only thought of scoring a goal. Each one wanted to conquer the whole world alone. It was a game of isolated talents.

Just like me, hundreds of kids born and brought up on that street wanted in their hearts to find the road to glory, to success, to money, to fancy cars, to beautiful women. They dreamed of having a passport to that miraculous world of big-time football, of stadiums exploding with cheers. Eleven against eleven, all the players with their football shoes, trainers, doctors, owners, masseurs, the stands, the fans, the reporters and television cameras.

It the first time I fell in love. It was an adolescent love, with all its childish wonders. The most innocent love in the world. We would walk hand in hand all up and down our chaotic street. We'd spend long stretches of time gazing into one another's eyes. Our souls were joined. We were accomplices in the desire that one day we could marry. Her name was Miriam.

We met each other in a garage dance on a rainy night. Decent folk were dancing there, together with thieves, drunks and prostitutes. A new dance ruled the street around that time: The Slow. We danced for hours without stopping. I lost track of the time. There had never been on the face of the earth a creature with such a beautiful shape. She was three, four, five times beautiful. Blessed the lips that seduced and won me so completely!

I would sweetly finger the locks over her ears, and stroke her hair. I would breathe in her cheap but wonderful perfume. I'd stare at her half-open lips, parted by passionate breathing. I felt a kind of shame at each step, but I was too involved to stop.

The blood in my veins was speaking, urging me to act. With every minute that passed I was more on fire. "I really like you," I exclaimed next to her charming ear. A deeply felt confession. It had been love at first sight. She asked softly, "Do you really like me?" It was a kind of a communion of childish joy.

That night we didn't even reach the first kiss. But love, shared by both, had appeared. When the music stopped, we stood there, holding each other, breathing deeply, dreaming too. Most of the guests had left. It was raining. It was raining a lot: a divine purification of our union. Two pure youngsters – whose lives had never known seductions, amorous affairs or erotic scenes – were passionately in love with one another.

Long before that my father had said that passion can blind a man. It's true. Miriam was the proof. As soon as I came back to myself, I realized that she was not as beautiful as she had seemed in the first days. She had a lovely face, but was a little overweight. She ate mainly bread and chocolate. Plus, she didn't know how to dress. She always wore the same clothes. Whoever saw her in a given month, saw her just as she was three or four months before or after. Nothing changed. In every season she wore woolen tights and heavy boots. And the summer was very hot.

My family always tried to keep me as far away as possible from the street gangs. Since I didn't belong to any gang, unkind kids gave me the nickname "Weakling." Of course I felt humiliated whenever they called me that. My father threatened to grab a pistol and kill the ones that crushed my self-esteem every day. Miriam would say, "Easy goes," and then, to console me, "Better a weakling alive than a dead tough." And she would add, "You are the one I like."

She studied in a school downtown, and was proud to be the best student in the class. Even though she was still quite young, she was already an intellectual, and people on our street really respected her. She belonged to an anarchist club and fought against the medieval living conditions on our street: thousands of miserable souls without decent food, without running water, without basic sanitation or electric light or access to education or the halls of justice.

Miriam helped men and women who didn't have the strength to organize themselves. She deftly took on the role of spokeswoman for the interests of the poor, the workers and the unemployed, in the name of international solidarity. At the first meeting I attended I was so moved that I cried. Standing on top of wooden boxes, a kind of improvised stage, Miriam showed people how they could fight against wrongs and stand up for their rights.

Sometimes she was sad because the political doctrines were completely outdated. The great debate in the society had a name: football. In the media, football had taken the place of politics and religion as the driving ideological force of nations.

The media and the marketing business had imposed an impressive dictatorial control over information. The space dedicated to the world of football suffocated every other kind of news, national and international: meetings of the United Nations Security Council, scientific discoveries, humanitarian activities, earthquakes, and every aspect of politics, economy, the arts and entertainment.

The main topics were banal aspects of football. The TV news on every channel concentrated on goals, team standings in the leagues, the hiring and firing of coaches, and so on. It was an unstoppable vicious circle. New programs and news reports about football generated more programs and more reports. There was nearly no time left to report on what was happening around the world. Miriam suffered from it.

Sometimes the tenor of her speech turned to liberating women from oppressive patterns based on gender roles. Miriam hated to see women with a broom in their hands and often used the slogan, "He should do the sweeping!" One time my mother came to hear one of her speeches. She got all worked up over what she heard. She came home grinding her teeth and grumbling that she was in favor of equality between men and women. Still, habit was stronger than any political idea. So as soon as she walked into the kitchen she immediately grabbed the broom and again began sweeping, sweeping, sweeping.

The bell on the tower of a far-off building has just rung five o'clock. Moonlight soaks the landscape with a silvery gleam. The wind has been calmer since last evening. Everything seems to be asleep. I am awake at the window, looking out at my street. I am cold. I feel hungry. The day is coming on, and with it the most extreme poverty. This is the most painful image I keep inside me from my childhood. I can never forget it. That street, just over a mile long, was my whole world.

A sea of wretched people was sheltering in buildings that ranged from six to ten stories high. Every foot of wall was covered with graffiti, with messages of death. One saw nothing but concrete, garbage, rusting sheet metal and torched cars. There was not a hint of earth or grass. Not a bird could be seen, not even a tree. All the wood was used in ovens on winter nights. To get warm, the beggars would grab onto the tall street lamps. I cannot find words crude enough to describe such a rude scenario, such a colorless life.

Many houses were worse than cattle wagons. Numerous families were crowded together in tiny rooms. They had no furniture. They slept on the floor. They ate on the window sill. Water dripped from the ceilings. All the stucco was peeling off. Some neighbors tried to help the poorest. But they were also poor and unlucky.

There had always been homeless people wandering around my street. They would fight amongst themselves for the best left-overs whenever the folks that lived there tossed a garbage bag out the window. It was as though coins were falling from the sky. Once I saw one wretch who had not a crumb of bread run tirelessly after a rat that was fleeing for its life, feeling in its ears the murderous breath of its pursuer.

The sky blended into lines of clothes hung out to dry. To really see the clouds and the sun you had to climb up onto the roof of a building. There the view of the city was stunning. The world was truly lovely. But not on my street. These images haunt me even today, like the trash swirling in the air and the swarms of flies.

Loads of people had no job. Every morning hundreds of men, their feelings numb, would eagerly thumb through pages of job ads in the newspapers. They were ready to suffer any kind of humiliation. They were eager to have a boss, even a despotic one, so long as he would make sure they had some rice on the table at dinnertime.

The women would argue back and forth from their balconies. Each one knew what was cooking in their neighbor's pot, so slight were the pickings. Mothers would work miracles with a drop of olive oil and a bit of beef. The smell of cooking was sometimes all the comfort that I had. Extreme poverty bred equality. I am a witness to that. A witness and a victim.

The masses, including of course the most simple among them, saw the quality of their lives get worse and worse. They had long since lost any hope of achieving a lifestyle with a minimum of human dignity. Meanwhile they all belonged to the human waves of mindless shrieking fans who dreamed of their idols scoring goals. The whole population was a hostage to football, even the poor. This illness infected millions of human beings, including those who had no hope in the future.

The mothers were usually friskier than their children. But not my mother, who always stood out for her modesty. She would spend her days at home, her eyelids swollen from lack of sleep, slaving from dawn until midnight, sweeping, cleaning, mending clothes, turning back worn-out collars, darning socks, and cooking whatever God allowed.

My father would leave every morning for his ill-paid job in a factory where the workers aged prematurely. As a child, he had lived in a village where people survived on the produce of the earth, in an atmosphere of real freedom, of working in the fields and enjoying innocent pleasures. The seeds of the earth had never taught him to act badly; the fruit from the trees had never stirred up an abject thought; nor had the flock awakened in him any feeling but love.

With dreams of wealth, of a lovely house and new car, he chose the city when he was still young, working glumly at a machine, until the factory whistle him set him free, day after day, week by week, every month, constantly.

My father's frustration was not unique. There were hundreds of people from the countryside on our street. All of them unhappy. They wanted to roll in the hay, smell the earth, walk on it barefoot. Nobody can imagine how happy those people would have been if they could just have a simple picnic or take off their shoes on fresh soil, without a garbage bin nearby.

There was no private life in my building. Constant screams from the stairwell and inside the apartments — separated by thin plaster walls — alerted us to the neighbors' problems: the husbands' fury, the lack of cash, the children's drug addictions, the abundance of cockroaches, lots of unpleasant things. And when there were no sounds in the night, we could hear the muted noises made by lovers. The nights were a torture. There was no such thing as a normal night.

When I left home every morning, I would see people that I didn't recognize sleeping on the stoop. People who felt no tenderness, no hope, whose eyes were grim. Women without shoes. Crippled men. Tears of despair. Suffering.

Groups of teen-age toughs born and bred in sinister buildings, where early on they had lost the notion of what is good or bad –since what society held to be crime was classified as virtue— spent the day playing billiards and smoking drugs. They would only leave the street when they meant to steal. Later they would return with what they had stolen, and squander that on gambling and tattoos, until they had to leave the street again, to steal some more.

There were huge numbers of prostitutes around. There had never been so much competition among them. Bad luck had launched hundreds of women in that career. Some offered their wares along the sidewalk; others lived in shabby apartments. By the time they were eight years old the boys on the street knew exactly what activity these ladies practiced. The word spread quickly among them.

Want and underdevelopment can produce lots of obese women. My cousin Jodie weighed over 200 pounds. In her youth she had given herself to life's impurities and became chained to habits and vices she could never shake off. She became a prostitute, caught a fatal venereal disease, and died young. Just as in a supermarket in an upscale neighborhood a piece of fruit handled by everyone is destined ineluctably to the trash bin, just so the prostitutes on my miserable street invariably ended up in a ditch of agony and death.

The pimps had extended their power far: they bought quite a number of buildings from their owners, become landlords and lords of a mass of the poor. Every day there were evictions for unpaid rent. Those who were evicted protested, but it did no good. Armed mercenaries would appear to enforce the will of the landlords. Brutal and frightening, it was they who governed the street. All the poor hated them but could do nothing.

I saw countless pimps going up and down the filthy steep stairways of the buildings on my street, one after the other, to collect the rent from those who didn't want to be kicked out immediately. How many times I saw beds and furniture thrown out of the windows. Convulsive crying followed many of these visits.

I remember walking up the street one New Year's Day. Festivity and sounds of celebration could be heard everywhere. But once again families were evicted and the heads of families shoved and pistol-whipped out of their homes. On the sidewalks you could see tables, chairs, mattresses, bedclothes, dirty dishes, crying babies, despair. Those families were so poor that they hadn't the courage to cry out loud. Anger was the prisoner of silence.

There were various gangs on the street, made of boys that had spent their childhood in depressing realities that nobody had prepared them for. They were not ready to judge what they saw with firm principles that might defend them from dishonest intentions and from committing the vilest crimes. The gangsters knew that although they could not change the world they could shake it to its roots. That in itself was gratifying.

Every morning the most alarming news would reach us from outside. There were constant bloody fights and pistol shots. Then screams, despair, weeping, ambulances. It was hard to guess who had died. I could be anyone. Criminals, prostitutes, flat-nosed bums, innocent people. It could be anyone.

You could barely find an honest home, or people who had decent living conditions and upbringing. Most of the homes were full of putrefaction and addiction. Virtue sank, completely crushed.

The children had the same schedule as the adults. It was common for them all to stay in the street until the day had fully dawned. I slept in a bed without a mattress or pillow. For years I rested my head on a card-board box, which little by little rodents were gnawing away. It was then that Uncle Herman came to my aid, giving me a brand-new cotton pillow. There and then I learned how so little can mean so much.

My uncle was a very ill-tempered man who seemed to hide behind his thin glasses, a personality charged with hatred and vengeance. "A man who's short: / venomous retort." In the street this proverb was used of him. He was known for always protesting against life. One day he got involved in a confrontation with a group of bikers. The outcome was that he got an awful stab wound in the stomach. My aunt, horrified at the scene, tried to stop the motorcycle rider with the black helmet and closed visor who had fatally knifed him, but she only succeeded in grabbing the air and saw the murderer roar off and vanish on the horizon. The poor woman cursed: she didn't even have a chance to look into the eyes of the man who had wrought the catastrophe she was living through at that moment.

The police only appeared on the street once a year, accompanied by troops with a helicopter following close behind, attentive snipers aboard. Rocks and garbage bags were hurled through the windows of dozens of buildings all at once. The enforcers of law and order always ended up thrashing about with their clubs as they retreated, confronted by furious cries of "Get out!" from a crowd of people.

That's what my street was like. It's still like that today.

On the street was a house that seemed like a castle, its façade in ruins, which everybody, even the most hardened criminals, was afraid of. The entryway was always half open and there was no lock, but nobody dared to peek inside. It was like a haunted house and around it there reigned a disturbing silence. Everything about it evoked the most impenetrable mystery. It was said that Baba Madri lived there, a wise man, a hundred years old, tall and upright, his head always covered, and that his eyes generated an incandescent clarity.

For many years nobody had seen him outside his home. This strange man was held in high regard by the older folks in the neighborhood, who said that he was already living in that house when they were born. His reputation was so old and mysterious that those who had recently arrived could not really understand it. And in relation to him, everyone had arrived recently.

I confess his enigmatic story intrigued me from childhood. Many times I asked myself why he had chosen to live like a mole, unable to distinguish day from night, remote from human interaction, alien to the real world. And for a long time I had been stirred by the urge to visit that house. Maybe the advice of a sage would be useful to me, a young man ignored by society, poorly fed and clothed, who had no means at all, much less enough to have a family, as I wanted [and desired]. I felt that I was condemned to be bitter and contrite forever, and that it was my own fault, since I had made no special effort to free myself from the bonds of the street or the chains of hunger. To visit Madri might mean life or death. I already lived in a scenario of death. I had nothing to lose.

On a rainy night I made up my mind to seek out Baba Madri. My legs shook, I even cried a little — out of humility. I was ready to confess to him all the sins of my life, leaving out nothing. I hadn't done anything seriously wrong in my life. My past included only some slightly shameful things that hardly deserved to be harshly censured.

I approached the house slowly, knocked on the door twice, shyly stuck my head into the hall and asked with a frightened voice if anybody was home. My question was answered by silence. The silence of books. Thousands of books, all piled up. Piles of books as tall as a tall man. It seemed a graveyard of books in a house whose inner spirit was unknown to the world. In me the scene evoked a timeless world. Still, I could just make out, at the end of the corridor, an eerie clarity emanating from two slowly burning torches. There was life in that house.

After a moment's hesitation I reorganized my thoughts and began to walk, step by step, through the rooms, corridors and stairwells of that odd dwelling. There was no furniture, no paintings, no plants. Just books. It was an extraordinary world of old rarities that could only have been collected by a seasoned bibliophile who was used to breathing dust. Time seemed to have come to an end there many centuries before. That mute silence seemed the infinite void of death.

In the hallways of that house I had to move sideways. I felt almost crushed between the walls lined with books piled high. It seemed a phantasy.

I entered a large room where a candelabrum stood on a massive stone table, as though presiding over a silent assembly.

The assembly of books. Pearls forgotten in time. Thick books, thin books; some huge, some small, piled in what seemed a disorganized way. It seemed that at any moment they might fall in an avalanche on top of me.

In front of me was a stone staircase. The flickering gleam of torches rendered the atmosphere truly frightening. I began, slowly and cautiously, to climb the steps and finally reached a narrow corridor.

I thought I heard breathing behind me. Appearing out of nowhere, Madri pointed his index finger in my direction. I fell down backwards and lay prostrate on the floor, motionless with fear, unable to confess to my own soul the strange thoughts running through my head. I could never have imagined meeting someone so disturbing.

In front of me, grave and austere, Madri appeared to be lost in his own thoughts. He had probably not seen another person for many years. Suddenly my host extended an arm towards me, grabbed me by the shoulder and lifting up my dead weight, set me in motion through the house, crossing all kinds of shadowy rooms. While I was being inexorably pulled along, in that world of books, I imagined the worst possible scenario. I would be gagged, tied to a bench and subjected to instruments of torture. Bones and ligaments snapped by stretching, nails torn out of my fingers, agonizing fire on my skin.

For a few moments tears fell from my eyes and I let out a long mournful sound. I surely didn't deserve such a severe punishment. Didn't I have a soul and tender feelings? Didn't human blood run in my veins? Didn't I have a family that was worried about me, an honest father, a hard-working mother, a girlfriend who spoke out for the rights of women?

The floor seemed to tremble under the heavy steps of this ancient man. He was tall in stature, with a black turban on his head and an enormous and majestic beard. Anyone would draw back with awe in his presence. An imposing, almost supernatural figure. I quickly understood why everybody on my street was afraid of the owner of that house.

Baba Madri came to a halt in a large room with two benches. At his command we sat facing one another. He seemed serene, concentrated. I looked at the room we were in, lighted only by the flames that danced around a torch. There was nothing there but a myriad of books and the benches we were sitting on. No furniture. Nothing to belie the look of sheer poverty.

"Who... who are you?" I asked foolishly, though I was the intruder.

"A simple man," he answered. "You would know me better if you had never met me."

"My name... my name is Daniel Malka," I said, staggered. "I came here tonight because I need good advice from someone who is old and wise." And then I blurted out: "I want to be rich and famous!"

"Fame is deadly. Obey the old proverb: 'Always stay in the shade, where there is light.'"

"What? The world is full of famous people who are happy. I believe every man wants to be recognized and respected."

"One day a snake began to chase a firefly. The firefly, when it felt the breath of its pursuer, looked back and said: 'My dear snake, I don't belong to your food-chain. And I never wronged you. Why do you want to devour me?' 'Because you shine.'"

I was silent for a moment. Then I asked plaintively, "Can't I at least have money?"

"Money won't do you any good. You don't know life, you have no judgement. Money in the hands of the ignorant evaporates. It will not give you life or bring you happiness.

"I don't agree. If I have money, I can save part of it and spend the rest to get things that I like."

"What things?"

"I don't know. Whatever's in fashion."

"Lots of style: poor in a while," goes an old saying. A rich man is not one who buys or has many material things but one who is content with what he has and happy with his wife."

"Well, if that's true, I'm on the right path. I'll marry Miriam, who's flawless. She's a fighter, she studies a lot, is responsible and hard-working. Maybe she's not that pretty. She's a little on the heavy side, and she has no taste in clothes. She dresses like a boy. But she's the girl I love."

"The most important thing is the soul, a divine spark, the energy beyond the five senses. Every soul is sent into the physical world with a double mission:

the overall mission of being at peace with God, and a specific mission. Often the soul spends its whole life without having the chance to find out what its special mission is. So it is reborn, one time or many times, until it fulfills its mission and reaches the necessary luster. We shall see if you find your path in this life. It's late. This conversation is over. I need to turn in. Peace, and good-bye."

I don't remember much more of this encounter with Baba Madri. I don't think I've ever fully understood it.

The next day my life changed abruptly and for years I livedasthoughthisconversationwiththatoldsagehadnever taken place.

On the football field of the old warehouse with no roof, the teams of blocks A and B were playing each other. They were made up of boys between 18 and 25 years old. I lived on block B and was the central midfielder of my team. Of all my teammates, I was the only one that had never been arrested. There was also someone on the block A team that had no criminal record. We were the only "clean" players – who had no contact with police, judges or prison guards.

Despite this situation, I should say that the clash between these teams of delinquents never degenerated into violence and pitched battles. There was manliness but a great deal of mutual respect among the players. "One-eyed" Jack, the club's main backer, did not allow brawls. He always watched the games very attentively. At the slightest sign of mischief among the players he would take his gun out of its holster and begin screaming that he was going to kill the lot of them. That day the game went badly for my team. Luck was not on our side. We lost. Jack liked the show and so did a few dozen spectators who were present in the warehouse. Among them was a stranger whom I had never seen on the street. He was impeccably dressed and sported a massive physique. He was almost seven feet tall, with a thick moustache, fat face and slow walk. His bulging stomach bespoke lots of business lunches and little physical exercise.

He walked over to me, looking friendly, and held out his right hand, evidently wanting to get to know me better.

"It's a great pleasure to meet you, Daniel. My name is Jason Parker, of the Parker family. I'm a football entrepreneur."

"Very pleased to meet you, sir."

"Can you tell me how old you are?"

"I turned 18 last month", I said.

"That's a good age. I've heard people talk a lot about you. That's why I came here to see a game. And you didn't let me down. You have talent and determination and your love of the game is obvious. I want you to be a professional football player. Would you like me to make a top line pro out of you?"

"Well, yes... (I stuttered). Of course!"

"OK, just give me some time. I need to wrap up a complicated deal with a club. It's a deal that involves several players. I am going to include you too. You'll have to do some try-out training sessions. I'm sure you'll grab the opportunity. It's a top club."

"I'm... I'm speechless. Am I really good enough to attract the interest of a top club?"

"I know if a player is worth the money or not. You never took vitamins – on the contrary, you look undernourished – and yet you run like a bull, you have strength, stamina and a good weight. You know how to use your shoulders, you control the ball well, you dribble and shoot with either foot. I'm convinced. If you do all this on this horrible pitch, full of bumps and holes, what will stop you from doing it on a football field with perfect grass? I know what I'm talking about."

"There are other good players here", I said. "Did you see the striker who played on our team today and was involved in a bunch of plays with me? He has really good technique. And the goalkeeper? He's very agile."

"There's no use trying to push the whole team on me. I'm not interested in anybody else. The striker has a good touch, but I know about his life. I have my informants. He's got several criminal cases against him in court. His youth is ruined. He'll soon be behind bars, smoking drugs and getting fat on prison food. And as for the goalkeeper, he's a greasy bungler who chose that position because he can't play any other. In the goal he can even play with his hands, to disguise his lack of skill."

That day, at the end of the afternoon, unaware of the security risks he was running, Jason stopped his big yellow car in front of the building where I lived, revving up the accelerator and honking with great fanfare. We had agreed to go have dinner in a restaurant. In front of the stares of several stunned locals I sat down in the passenger seat, put on the seatbelt and swelled with pride. I had never been in such a comfortable and fast car before. It was my first trip on a wingèd horse.

With tires screeching, the car took off at high speed, leaving behind a trail of smoke and devouring the pavement. Everybody came to the window and talked about the event. Jason was well-known after all. He was a public figure in the world of football. The newspapers fought each other to get an interview with him. In a wink of an eye the news that I might be hired by a big football team spread through the street like wildfire.

We got to the restaurant. A very fancy kind of restaurant whose existence I could not have imagined: with an inner garden, luxury furniture, gilded bathrooms, and an army of elegantly dressed employees ready to wait on any customer, even on me. Never in my whole life had I been waited on. This was the first time.

Jason's wife was already there waiting for us. Her name was Alina. A small woman, with full hips and breasts, large shoulders and bony knees. She was a bit tired, and looked bored. She appeared to have little patience for her husband's frenetic behavior.

Jason was a regular at that restaurant. It was as though he were part of the furniture. The other customers knew him. He walked from one end of the restaurant to the other showing off his keen sense of humor.

"What has a hundred legs but doesn't walk?" He asked this question in a loud voice, addressing everyone there. Nobody could answer. "Fifty paralytics!" he finally said, laughing loudly while he spilled his beer down his tie.

I quickly learned that Jason was a loudmouth. He would have been afraid of the very words "Gag him!" His enormous head made everyone in the room wonder at him, and his moustache inspired onlookers to imagine a labyrinth of galleries with fantastic outlines.

Without stopping for a moment, he continued to monopolize completely the conversation there, telling how one day he had managed to go to a barbecue restaurant and buy quails without paying for them.

"I ordered a chicken and then asked the waiter to make it two quails instead. I turned around and walked out the door carrying them under my arm. The waiter ran after me saying that I hadn't paid for the quails. I said, 'I didn't pay for them because I exchanged the chicken for them.' 'But you didn't pay for the chicken!' he said. 'I didn't pay for the chicken, but I'm not taking the chicken with me!' And I left." Ha-ha-ha-ha. That was some trick!

At that moment a tray of rice and beans with roast veal arrived. Jason could not refrain from jabbing his thumb into the rice, and then he said jokingly:

"It's hot! Yum!"

Once upon a time, he said, his mother had advised him to open a butcher shop. "It's a business with a future, and you won't go hungry!" He recalled his mother's firm reaction when he told her that he wanted to go into the football business.

For a few moments I imagined him putting on a white apron stained with bovine blood and with the residue of skin embedded in his fingernails. His only work-tool would be a huge cleaver and he would have no greater problems with the neighborhood than the occasional question of a sliver of fat too much or too little.

Midnight. The restaurant was completely empty except for our table. Now we were being a nuisance. The waiters remained at their posts, expectant. Time was passing. Jason stayed seated, talking on with a melancholy tone. He was not well. He had already drunk two bottles of wine.

He swallowed one more gulp and suddenly got up walking unsteadily towards the W.C. But he went in the wrong door. The sound of flushing echoed through the room. A female employee of the restaurant shot out of the bathroom like a rocket, very flustered, and fled at full speed through a maze of corridors that led to the kitchen.

It was not easy to sleep that night. My mind would not stop imagining different scenarios: the moment that I became a professional athlete, my goals, my perfect passes. A neighborhood kid with a swelling chest, respected by the world press, covered with honors and with money. Football would allow me to engrave my name in History, to have countless admirers, a beautiful wife, a new car, a house with a pool, expensive clothes and money in the bank. Was this fantasy or reality?

A few days later my greatest desire was realized. First thing in the morning. A mist had already covered my street when I woke up, feeling heavy, fighting against a strange sluggishness that invaded my body, and from which I emerged painfully. I went over to the window, trying to organize my thoughts, and as soon as I fixed my eyes on the street I saw something that filled me with satisfaction. Jason was standing in front of my building, signaling effusively in my direction.

I ran down the stairs, breathless and ill-kempt. I fell into his arms and he told me what I wanted to hear.

"Are you ready to take a trip with me today, kid? We leave tonight. I'll be taking you far away. Tomorrow you'll do some training and take medical exams. You'll get the green light from the coach. I've got business with him. Your life will never be the same. You won't see this miserable street again any time soon."

At that moment I felt a mixture of joy and sadness. Even though I was about to fulfill my dream of leaving behind the boundaries of the street on my way to a better future, I began right there to miss my parents and Miriam. There might be richer, friendlier and more polished parents than mine. There might also be women who were finer and prettier and more charming than Miriam. But they were my parents and my girlfriend.

Noticing my sad look, Jason (who a few moments before was showing signs of apprehension that he could not hide) quickly took a position on the matter, in a brusque tone.

"Make up your mind, kid. Things in life are simple. The rich buy; the poor sell themselves. Nothing else to do. If you're proud or sensitive, you'll end up as a failure. I know it's tough to say goodbye to your family. You're bound to them by the roots. You leave your girlfriend behind too. It's sad. But believe me: distance will make separation easier. In not too long you'll stop suffering. I've had lots of experience with kids that cried when they left home. I lifted them all out of the gutter. I found them dirty and I washed them. They had no clothes, so I clothed them. They were hungry; I fed them. But I have rights too. Men are tamed with food, clothing, and vanity. I take them out of poverty, but I insist that they play well and value their own worth, without moping around corners to cry because they miss their parents, their friends and their girl."

This argument did not persuade me. It wasn't very different from the one that pimps on the street used with prostitutes at the beginning of their career. Still, I couldn't lose that opportunity. I packed my clothes in two sacks and took leave of my parents with great emotion. I also said goodbye to Miriam, whom I had in the meantime called and who was crying over my departure. I promised her that I would come back rich and marry her. I promised her that one day we would have our own home. And I left.

And so began a long car-trip, crossing bridges, rivers, mountains and highways, ending up in a large and cosmopolitan city. I didn't repent of my adventure. A year later I would be a famous football player, known the world over and worth my weight in gold. I had realized my dream.

I signed a contract that was good for six seasons —with a preference clause for four more— with a highly professional club that had structures and resources infinitely better than those of the "little club" of ragged amateurs in the old warehouse on my street. I now was part of a team where players, coaches, managers, administrators, doctors and masseurs all had their roles. I was at long last in a world of miracles.

On the pitch in the stadium the grass was beautiful. It seemed like a smooth green carpet of the highest quality. I could use my abilities and strengths to the limit. I would never again find myself falling helplessly into old boards and barrels of cement at the edge of the pitch. No longer would I get home with my knees and elbows scraped up. I had left poverty and misery behind.

I remember as if it were today the moment when I met the coach, Anthony Baldwin. He came over to me with a friendly look after the first workout.

"Good morning, Daniel. I'm glad to meet you. Liked what I saw today. You have stamina. You're strong. You pass well. You don't hold onto the ball too much. Keep that up. Use your head. Football is more than sweating hard. It's also inspiration and intelligence. Keep passing like that, energize the team. That way the ball moves around more than the players. And it doesn't get tired. Although it might lose some air."

"I understand sir" (I said humbly).

"Jason Parker spoke to me. Yes, he believes you've got real skill. I'm going to help you. I'll do my part as well as I can. And you do your part. That's a fair division of labor: each of us does half the work."

"I'll take that deal, sir. Much honored. I'll do my best. I was born poor. I'm not proud. I'll be here running twelve hours a day if I have to."

"I don't want you to run that long. Part of your work is learning. Another part is working out. Another is resting. Now I'll give you your first lesson. What do you most urgently need to learn?"

"I don't know", I said.

"What is the first great secret of players that hold the masses spellbound with football: Feinting? Touching the ball? Scoring goals? The answer will surprise you. You need to know how to tie your shoes. Think about it. Look at me. The shoe has to be tight but comfortable on the foot. You have to lace it up like this. Now watch how I do it. Pay attention. Like this..."

Baldwin was a demanding man, methodical down to the last detail. Every week he handed out dossiers to the players, dossiers about the characteristics of our opponents. He insisted that his players study. Plus he had a very peculiar style.

To keep the players' attention during his talks he would chop his phrases in half and suddenly change the dynamics of his voice. For example, if he wanted to tell the players to focus on marking the other teams' players, he would say softly, "Focus..." and then brusquely, screaming, foaming at the mouth with fury, "Focus on marking your man!"

His pregame pep-talks were real theater. The players had to perk up their ears to hear certain words, but were nearly put to flight when the coach reached the second part of his instructions. And there was always a war-cry at the end: "Go get 'em," he would say softly. And then after a slight pause he would scream with all the power in his lungs: "Go get 'em like Tarzans!"

In those early days I tried to train as hard as possible, to win a place of my own on the team. Like all street kids I was born to compete at the limits of my strength and tolerance for pain. Yes, I trained a lot. At night I would talk on the phone for hours with Miriam. I would carefully describe to her my day-to-day life. One of my most common complaints, which she always listened to patiently, was about the haughty attitude of the team's most senior players, who formed a kind of elite clique, impossible to infiltrate. Miriam referred to them as "pressure-cooked capitalists."

After practice sessions these older players would have lunch together in luxury restaurants, with wine flowing around the table. The younger athletes could not participate in these get-togethers. The conversation invariably turned to fine cars and amorous conquests. Jason was right. In one of his wise tirades he had said:

"Daniel, the enemy is there in the showers with you; your opponents are on the other team!"

Although the team was made up of very accomplished and experienced players, in a short time I won my place among the substitutes and then became a regular starter. I confess that my trainer also helped me along. The regular starting eleven belonged to three agents: Jason and two others, who split the cake of future transfers with the coach and the president of the club. Even if the club contracted real stars during the summer transfer season they wouldn't win a spot among the starters. Instead they would spend the whole years with the substitutes or playing on the B team. That is what usually happened.

At any rate, my displays of skill vanquished the mistrust that attaches to a player who hasn't played in a club before, a player with no résumé at all. Sports writers recognized how well I played. An illiterate youngster who had been a zero in society had conquered a new world, in a club where everybody could dream of becoming famous.

In a newspaper interview, the coach Anthony Baldwin spoke of me like this:

"Daniel is a real piranha on defense. He charges his opponents with ferocious drive. And when he gets the ball he either passes it or passes the other man. He doesn't pass both. (He smiled). On attack he designs magnificent shots on goal, head upright, the ball glued to his foot with a broad vision of the game. He delivers the ball to the right spot at the right moment. When the ball comes to him he already knows where it's going. It's a gift. And he also has a powerful kick from medium distance, with his right or left foot, and he often breaks into the area to finish a play which he began. He's a first class player and he's going to be a world class star."

Soon I managed to be invited to lunches with the older players. Stardom had arrived. I began to be thronged by enthusiastic fans. Fan letters filled my mailbox every morning. I bought myself an expensive pen to sign autographs in notebooks and diaries. It was great to play football and get paid for it and be idolized into the bargain.

Strange: a football game lasts ninety minutes, divided into two parts, measured by the referee, the weakest person on the field of play. In the middle of twenty-two warriors, eleven on each side, stuffed with vitamins and ready to eat the grass if that's what it takes to win, stood a referee in pants and sneakers, as frail as a cup of milk.

Television cameras were spread throughout the stadium, inside and out. Behind the goals photographers clustered, so they wouldn't miss any part of the game. Medical teams were alert too, in case an athlete got injured. Even the ball-chasers appeared to be nervous. Every game seemed the most important moment of their lives.

Dirty words were the regular currency of players on the team. They take on great importance in football. It may seem unbelievable, but I heard more dirty words spoken while playing football than during my whole childhood and adolescence among a thousand thieves.

At the beginning my team-mates had thought me a dolt. For them, to be tough meant saying a bunch of dirty words and telling risqué stories. Later, when I earned star status, I won the respect of the other players. When I approached they would suspend their piquant stories, saying to one another, "Here comes Daniel; let's change the topic."

I still have a cassette with the TV coverage of the first goal I scored for the club. It was a long powerful kick. There were two commentators, both contentious. That day each was rooting for one of the teams. Here's a transcript of how they covered the decisive moments:

"Ladies and gentleman, we are in the twenty-fourth minute. The game is even. The crowd is rooting for the home team. Daniel gets the sphere just outside his own area. He takes off. He sees Foxman unmarked, but doesn't send him the ball. He's moving forward. Passes midfield, veers towards the center. Gets by one opponent, another, speeds up, and ... he's mowed down! Savagely mowed down by Michael Green! A really ugly foul."

"That didn't seem like a foul to me" (said the other commentator).

"What? That was a shameless foul. Daniel was simply mowed down. He's hurt. Look at him twisting in pain."

"I thought he was clearly faking a foul. Daniel exaggerates a bit in this kind of situation. He's a fine player, but sometimes throws fits. Let's wait for the replay."

"Ok, here is the replay. Daniel feints once, feints twice, and while he's gliding down the center... right here. Here it is. He is literally rammed by two defenders at the same time, brought down by two pairs of feet. Clearly a foul. This should be a booking. Let's see what the referee does. He's got a card in his hand. The question is: will it be red?"

"Red? Red for what?"

"For what? The ref only showed Michael Green a yellow card. His brain seems off kilter today."

"Excuse me, but I don't agree. I think the ref made two mistakes on the same play. He called a foul that didn't happen and penalized an athlete who had done nothing wrong."

"The ref understandably doesn't want to wreck the game. We'll still in the first half."

"Let's watch the replay again, pal. Ok, here it is. This shows that I'm right. Daniel guides the ball... right here he feints for the second time and realizing that he is going to have it taken away cleanly he deftly leaps over his adversary and throws himself against the turf. There's minimal contact, that's inevitable in a fast game like this. I'll go further. I don't think there was enough contact to bring him down."

"Oh no? Daniel is on the ground surrounded by medical staff."

"It'snotsurprisingthathefellbadly.Needstolearnhowto fall better."

"Excuse me for telling you, but you seem not to understand football — at all. Only here in this country could a commentator deny such an obvious foul."

"Are you talking about me? Have you no shame? In any other country a commentator wouldn't take sides the way you do. I may have to talk with the channel's stockholders. I think you can continue the commentary by yourself. Good bye! I am sorry to our viewers, but I can't take this jerk. I'll be back soon. Bye-bye!"

"I apologize to our viewers for this sad spectacle. Some people want to take the players' part and get into the action. Well... anyway... let's see... We all have a right to have bad days. Ok, the game goes on. The massage is over and the masseur is leaving the field. Daniel is finally back on his feet. Limping a bit, but he seems ready for the free kick. Yes, he's going to take the kick. He's a good forty meters from the goal. He takes the ball. He may try to drive it straight in. In the last game he tried to score from this far out and almost hammered it home. This youngster has a powerful kick. But Obama, the goalkeeper, seems unafraid of anything. He's gesturing with his arms that he does not want a barrier. At nearly seven feet tall he is a giant in that goal, with hands of iron. This is a serious moment. Daniel is taking it all in. Steps back one, two, three, four, five steps. He's focused. Kicks the turf twice. He's gonna go for it. The fans are twisting their hands in suspense. No wonder. Daniel runs at the ball, let's fly... and what a bomb! Goal! What an incredible goal by Daniel. What an amazing goal!"

This was the best period in the history of the club, which went down a path of stupendous victories, filling its tireless fans with pride, enriching the great history of the city itself. The fans, it was said, were going wild expecting fresh and resounding wins. On the days when there were games they would line up early and fill all the routes to the stadium. They felt no cold or hunger. That didn't matter. They just wanted to see their idols race around the field, feinting and drilling the ball into the nets of the other team's goal.

The stadium parking lot seemed like a car-show for luxury automobiles. The club's security people would not let a modest car park there. At the end of the lot were twenty fairly good cars that the club's official backer had put there for the players. But they didn't want those cars for themselves or for their wives. They only wanted the fanciest cars, which they would paint as if they were racing cars, with their names on the door, as though they were rally drivers.

I remember the day when I opened a bank account for the first time in my life. It quickly grew. So much money. I didn't know what to spend it all on. Miriam said to save it. I asked my teammates for advice. I splurged and bought a new house, cars, clothes, watches, so many things.

I used to leave the stadium revving up a yellow Ferrari, and so became a more attractive target for gorgeous women, sensual and provocative, who thronged the world of football. Beautiful, voluptuous and desirable women. No fat on them, no chocolates in their purses, or complicated political conversations or greasy hair. Everything about them was spellbinding. Which was the most seductive, the most tempting? Trees brimming with juice-filled fruit just waiting to be plucked. By me.

Miriam, with her extra pounds and boy's clothing could not stand up to so many beauties. Going against all my earlier plans, in a night and a day I broke off my engagement to her and married a professional model named Renata Bianchi. In time I'll tell you the tragic double sorrow that followed my decision.

At the end of that first year the team won the national championship. Renata thought I should get a big salary raise. I called Jason and we set up a meeting with the club president. Just the three of us.

The president, Bartholomew, was considered an implacable negotiator, ready with an answer to everything, while Renata had no regard for niceties in her behavior or manners.

With facile speech and slang always on the tip of her tongue, she was ready to threaten and insult anyone who spoke out against her, no matter who it was, at home, at the hairdresser's, in a shoe store, restaurant or police station.

Naturally, I thought that Jason would lead the meeting. But Renata would not let him. She began to speak, turning to the president in a foul mood.

"Hello. What Daniel makes is nothing. It should be double or triple that. It's thanks to him that the team won the national championship."

"Not at all" (said Bartholomew). "There are sixteen men on our team, including substitutes. Not just Daniel. He's a great player. We really respect him. But his success depends on the rest of the team. And none of them has asked for more money."

"If the club doesn't wanna raise his salary he can look for a new club. Here or abroad. There's no lack of takers."

"Not gonna happen. He has a five-year contract" (said the president, with some impatience).

"We'll break it."

"On what basis, Renata? You can't do that."

"Who cares on what basis? Our lawyer will come up with a reason."

At this point Jason tried to intervene:

"Oh Renata, you're not being fair with the president. Really..."

"Be quiet (Renata shot back). I don't wanna hear a peep out of you today. What I want is for them to be fair to Daniel."

"There are laws in this country (said the president). And there are rules in this club. Things just don't work the way you want them to."

"If it comes down to it, Daniel will refuse to play. He makes as much soaking up the rays on our poolside at home. Why should he play? Stop kidding us."

"Be careful. What you're saying makes no sense."

"You be careful. Look at yourself in the mirror. A lecher in a fancy suit and shoes is still a lecher. I'm gonna walk out of here screaming that you're doin' it with the coach's wife. I've got proof. Photos. I'm warning you: there are reporters near the elevator. I'll tell 'em everything. You choose. I'll give you two minutes. Not a second more."

Renata spoke this words while shaking a pen in the president's face. And she did it with such fury that he jumped backwards like a frightened cat. Jason and I were petrified and followed every word of that stormy conversation.

Everything turned out well. Renata and I left the meeting with a signed contract with a raise that doubled my salary and annual phased increases after the second year. Jason stayed for a few minutes to speak with the president, to apologize, I suppose, for the way the meeting had veered off in a direction that he didn't at all want. After that scene the president never again agreed to let a player bring his wife to a meeting.

Offers from other clubs, in the same country and abroad, stared pouring in. Jason told me right away that there were two offers that I couldn't walk away from and that it was time to leave this club. But after meeting with the president he quickly changed his mind. I had the sensation that it was Jason and not me that bettered his contract with the club. I even thought of telling Renata about my suspicions. Good thing I didn't do it. She would have clawed Jason's bloated face with her nails.

I signed several advertising contracts over the years. In the photo sessions Jason would usually stay half-hidden behind a screen, peeking out and making more or less meaningless comments, like "Very good, Daniel!" or "Nice shot, better than the last!" – comments that let him take a 30% slice of every contract.

Renata loved money. When she found out how big a percentage of the money Jason was making off the contacts she got furious and went after him like a lioness.

"You cheat, you're just exploiting him, you're stealing bread from our table."

"But I was the one that set up the contract" (said Jason, outraged).

"I don't see anybody taking photos of you. You're an ugly fatso. My Daniel is the one everybody wants to see. You can have 1% of the advertising contract, I can accept that. But 30% is too much. No, absolutely not."

"Ok, Renata. I won't bother setting up advertising contracts for Daniel. I had three more in my briefcase. Big fat sums. It's your decision."

"I take back what I said" (replied Renata). "You can have 30%."

Because of how I played on the pitch, and the will to win that I always showed and my dashing style of fighting to win, energetically urging my teammates on, I was nicknamed "The Gladiator." Although this name was given me by the team, the media —which always liked sensational words— quickly took it up. News reports about me were scattered around the universe. On magazine covers I appeared in drawings as an extraordinary muscular figure, brandishing a shield in an epic pose that thrilled the masses.

The coach was always at me, urging me on more and more.

"Daniel, balls at midfield have to be yours. They all have to be yours, whether they're high or not, fought over or not, whoever's on the other side, anywhere. Understand? They are yours. You are The Gladiator."

"There are opponents who play with their elbows" (I said). "I have to protect myself. I can't just look at the ball."

"The referee and the TV are there. They see. I'm on the bench ready to scream at the ref if I have to. Head the ball. Don't be afraid. It's not a bomb. It's not going to blow your head off. Don't ever hesitate. Ever."

"Ok, I'll do it."

"In my days as an athlete everything was much worse. There were no railings around the pitch or police or television or ambulance or referee worthy of the name. The ground seemed like cement. The other team's fans spat on the players during the match. Nobody wanted to play on the flanks. Once I was hit on the head with an iron when I tried a cross at the goal line. Another guy got knifed. But it's not like that anymore. The stadiums are full of police and security guards. There's a barrier between the crowd and the players. In-house TV catches offenders. The turf is a soft carpet. Even the slouches play well. The ball keeps on getting lighter. So many things have changed. It's easy to play that way. No reason at all to be afraid, Daniel!"

Even now I dream of the stadium full of ecstatic fans, applauding when I took the ball from the other team, or made perfect passes, or scored goals. I was a public personality at the height of my fame, power and wealth. I lived with a sense of superiority in relation to the players on the other team, or for that matter all of humankind. A feeling based on kicking the ball and on showing off my clothes, cars, homes, vacations, watches and sunglasses. And I had a fine wife who was a prestigious model.

On match-days the team bus, always followed closely by police cars and TV helicopters, was parked in the lot of the stadium where the game was going to be played. The fans at the end, held back by a tight security cordon, were jumping for joy when it was a home game, or else shaking with rage. I was usually the first player to come out of the bus, right after the president and the masseur. I would do it with a petulant air, wax in my hair, and huge headphones in my ears, like a god in a sweat-suit.

The photo-journalists hovered around me like flies, trying to find the best angles for a shot. The TV cameras followed my steps with dedication, broadcasting to the country and the world the image of footballer player in a daze, without any sense of taste, only interested in contracts, goals, hairstyles, pop music and squandering money. I remember one day I puffed out my chest so far that I almost fell over backwards.

Every day I had to deal with crazed fans celebrating the immortal feats the team was pulling off. An endless personality cult was gathering around me.

One day I decided to go to a mall to buy purple shoes to replace a pair that had been torn. I walked into a store and before I could even get to the counter I was carried out on the shoulders of fans, like a bullfighter on a day of triumph. They grabbed me and tossed me into the air, singing a song they often sang in the stadium: "Gladi-, gladi- gladiator! Gladi-, gladi-, gladiator!"

The typical fan or fanatic didn't care if I was sometimes busy or ill or missed my parents or if my wife was interrupting my rest or if false friends were constantly pressuring me or if invidious neighbors had scratched my car. All that and much more was part of my daily life and affected my state of mind and my income. But no fan cared if I had a life beyond the rectangle of grass on which we played. For him, I was merely a machine and always ought to play the same way, with the same strength and speed, the same technique and state of mind.

I had no peace anywhere, not even at home. A woman who sold banners set up shop in front of where I lived. I think she'd always done that kind of work. At least she looked like she had. Whenever I went in or came out she would scream with all his lungs, "Go, Daniel!" "Go, Gladiator!"

How often I got into fights with paparazzi. They would follow me everywhere. They'd park in front of my home and knew my every step from the banner peddler. Then they would push back the seat of the car and stay there, watching, waiting for a good chance to shoot photos. If I merely greeted a neighbor, as a question of manners, there would be headlines like "Caught in the Act" or "A New Romance" or "The Gladiator betrays Renata," etc.

This excessive exposure caused me a lot of emotional wear and tear. I did everything I could not to fall into disgrace in front of the press. I took vitamins in industrial quantities and on the pitch tried to display the kinds of good moves that had won me stardom and good repute. I had no time to breathe and live. Fame had become an endless nightmare.

Many times Jason gave me advice on how to relate to the fans and the press.

The way of the masses is the way of oxen. Laugh when it suits you, but stay out of their way. Otherwise they'll pull out your hair to make relics or to burn it, depending on the whim of the moment.

The press conferences I took part in, sometimes still breathing hard from the miles I had run during the game, were truly depressing spectacles. I couldn't even express myself as I wished to, and came across as obviously incoherent, incapable of speaking clearly or logically about any serious matter.

There was hardly a response of mine that didn't stem from some kind of ignorance. I used a characteristic tone that always served, like an algebraic formula, to answer all the reporters' questions: "uh-uh-uh". Then I would add some unimportant phrase to this savage noise, such as, "The only thing that matters is winning" or "We're going to play to win" or "We want those three points" or "We have to keep our head high and think about the next game."

I knew a veteran reporter who specialized in long interesting interviews with unintellectual players He interviewed me several times. He would ask questions in long phrases, intelligent and well-phrased, to which I would respond with a "Yes" or a "No." Then he would attribute to me all the words in the questions. Anyone that read these interviews in the newspapers would be fooled. Naturally, I was not responsible for those long and well-structured replies.

One day another reporter, already in a sweat, lost his head with me and told me he was going to quit that line of work.

"That's enough! I am sick of this job. My old mother was right. I deal with brutes. Not that all men have to be thinkers, but all this intellectual poverty is too much. Today I'm going to abandon the life of sports reporter."

"But (I said, trying to dissuade him) think about the beauty of the game, the overflowing stadiums, all the goals that you could still report during the rest of your career."

"Don't talk to me about that", he said. "I'm sick of childishness. You know what the players do when they score goals. Have you any idea how ridiculous it is? I'm too old to put up with kids who run around making their shirts into windmills or assume artistic poses or crawl around on their hands and knees like puppy dogs. Makes me angry."

"Lots of learned people go on TV to defend the football clubs they love" (I said, in defense of my profession).

"I don't want to hear about it (he said). It's the height of absurdity."

"But why?" I asked. "There are countless TV programs with panels made up of fans from the best clubs in the league."

"What a joke! They're like seated warriors. Steady in their faith, steady in their studio chairs. They nearly get into fistfights with each other, live on-air, remembering "incidents" from old games and interpreting off-sides and yellow cards according to the needs of their clubs. If the fans of one club say 'Yes' to everything, the fans of the other clubs all say 'No', with no respect from any of them for ethics or truth. Sometimes they practically grab each other by their ties to make their points. So long, Daniel. So long to this horrific world. I finally feel free. So long."

It was a sad day for me. I felt humiliated, but not guilty. I had spent my childhood and adolescence like a stray dog. Anybody in my shoes would turn out the same or worse. Probably would have been arrested or killed.

Many of those known as cultured men in the modern world would never have been able to survive in the underworld. They don't have the culture for that. They don't know what it is to divvy up one piece of beef per week or dream every night of flames, fire and screams. They don't know what it is to face an early death and the diseases that inevitably arise in impoverished homes. They have never felt the sensation of victory that comes just from not breathing garbage, from having bread to eat every morning, or from just being able to put on warm clothes.

I'm familiar with all that. It's my culture. A special culture. No reporter or interviewer has ever asked me about all that. All their questions revolve around the ball, the game, the team or the state of the turf. What would I be able to tell them? What would a renowned philosopher say? There really is nothing worth saying.

One day Jason said something to me that I never forgot.

"Daniel, they accuse you of having no culture. But you should ignore people that mock you. You were born into disgrace and now you are as popular as any star of politics, the movies, music or any other field of human endeavor. The people need you. They don't just want bread. They need the circus too. Politicians take care of the bread, badly for the most part. And you take care of the circus, for the most part well. What do you do for society? A lot. Your job is to take shots to the delight of the crowd. Men of culture wish they could be football players. They are failures in today's world, praying for somebody like you to throw some coins on the table. The same goes for lawyers, doctors, engineers, architects. They'd be loyal to you for a handful of bills. You're the one that's a star, not them. Congratulations! You have the world at your feet."

"Money isn't everything in life. And there are men a whole lot richer than I am", I said.

"Sure there are. But what is their life like? It's buying and selling at a small profit. No exercise is more banal than that. Any fool knows how to do it. It's a matter of luck, skill and timing. It works for some people. You've done a lot more than buy cheap and sell at a profit. You came from an underworld full of hunger. And thanks to your strength and physical smarts you became a man known around the planet. The rest is nothing but words."

During my whole career my mind was sailing through a sea of incomprehension. I didn't know if I was "The Weakling" or "The Gladiator" or both. I was certainly an idol of the masses, very limited and not up to the task, thanks to the world of the street where I grew up. And I was completely unprepared to deal with an excess of money or with self-interested people around me or with an excess of fame.

One day a rumor spread that the opposing team had ordered a toad to be buried alive in the turf of our stadium. In a normal world that fact would at most merit a shrug of the shoulders. But in the world of football a simple toad can lead to the squandering of millions.

The president of the club, who was very superstitious, ordered the whole pitch dug up, so that it looked like an enormous potato plantation. The body of the tiny animal never appeared and they had to implant a fresh carpet of turf in record time. Later I found out that the whole affair was just a trick by Renata who had created the false rumor.

The players were also very sensitive to questions of good and bad luck, blessings and curses. They always entered the stadium with the right foot and stuck amulets in their pants or shirt. The one who put those ideas in their heads was Archibald, the masseur. I myself played with a rabbit's foot on my shin.

The masseur once said in the locker room that he had supernatural powers and could guide the ball with a look. One day, the other team hit the bar with the ball and he began to jump with joy on the bench.

"Yes! It was me that blocked that goal! Yes!"

On match days the masseur's girlfriend, who was tall like him but more chunky and full-breasted, used to carry in a black hen. The role of this bird of ill-omen was to lodge behind the opponent's goal. At halftime, when the teams switched from one side of the field to the other, the masseur's girl and the hen would leave the stadium and then come in from the opposite side, casting a spell on the entire scenario.

The players adored the masseur. And they credited him with some of their wins. One day before a game against a strong team Archibald used a trick to give us the edge. He managed to divert everybody's attention and slipped into the other team's locker room with the ease of a monkey and stole their football shoes. It was a real scandal. During a month the press spoke of little else.

The other team lost badly and after the game their players ended up with blisters on their feet from using new shoes, which had been hastily purchased in a specialty shop. In our locker room, on the other hand, delight reigned supreme and corks popped from champagne bottles. Archibald was carried shoulder high and tossed into the air.

The relationship between our coach and the masseur was not overly friendly. Archibald often became involved in matters that properly belonged to the coach and since he could not choose the starting eleven directly he tried to do it indirectly, orchestrating intrigues full-time, to the point where he created little "groups" that undermined the collective spirit that the coach tried so hard to forge.

Before games the coach would sprinkle rock salt in the dressing room to ward off bad vibes. The masseur thought this madness, a senseless superstition. He blindly believed in the power of the hen.

Unfortunately for the coach, who wanted to get rid of him, the masseur had a close friendship with the club president, who was also fanatical about amulets. So "Him or me" didn't work.

One day this cauldron boiled over during a match. After the coach saw one of the defensemen, a friend of the masseur, roll over the other team's striker with the force of a tank, so that he had to be carried off on a stretcher, he turned to his assistant, Sam Gere:

"This is what happens when our players wear horseshoes for good luck. I am sick of having witch-doctors around."

The masseur realized that this was addressed to him, and answered:

"Did you want something? You don't understand anything about good luck. Go do your work, jerk!"

The fans behind the goal near the bench all burst into laughter. Even one of the referees, who knew of the tensions between coach and masseur and had stayed there listening, thought it funny.

The two of them thrust out their chests and began to insult each other. The squabble did not end well: it got physical. Nobody in the stadium was watching what went on the field anymore. There was another "game" now: the one on the bench. The boxing match between the two men only ended when the cops got there and took both the coach and the masseur to the police station.

The biggest celebrity on the team was Foxman, even though sports reporters sometimes favored me. His dribbling was as amazing as any I had ever seen. He fought with matchless energy at every point in a game. He was the very image of stubbornness, stamina and zeal. He had a truly powerful kick, was a consummate header, and could take on any pair of midfielders in the world. He was a prodigious, unstoppable force.

When he was a child Foxman used to run naked like a rabbit through fields and woods. He felt uncomfortable in clothing. He couldn't deal with it. Maybe because of that he didn't pay much attention to hygiene. I say that with good reason. When he began to play on our team he was knew in the city and unfamiliar with everything. I often gave him a lift. What a torture! A sharp smell of earth and rot emanated from his clothing, forcing me to fight hopelessly against that unexpected foe. He was a country boy, always a bit dirty, and had probably never taken a proper bath.

One day the team captain called a bunch of players to the shower room and tried to find a way to convince Foxman to wash better and use deodorant. The plan was never put into practice. When the masseur found out what was in the works, he let everybody know that Foxman could never smell good without the team losing all its games. The team was obviously afraid and had to put with that foul odor.

The team doctor would often appear in the locker-room to show the athletes (for the nth time) a long list of forbidden foods and a shorter list of foods they could eat. For the younger guys, who were eager to try any dish, it was no fun studying the first list.

Other times the coach would appear with an air of wisdom about him, his chin resting on his right hand, likewise concerned about the athletes' health, but for other reasons. What worried him were their nighttime outings. His tutees' ability to give their best might be seriously affected by nights out and nocturnal vices.

Some players would get shaky legs, knowing that they were being examined. The whole city was in the hands of the club coaches, managers and directors. Detectives, security people and hardcore fans followed the players all the time, day and night. There were paid informants in every nightclub, in the casinos and restaurants and in the world of high-priced escorts.

The directors were tipped off at once anytime a player decided to have fun at night, defying the explicit rules set by the club. Sometimes they would beat him up. When the transgressor got home in the wee hours of the morning, smelling of smoke and booze, he might get half a dozen punches, the work of hooded men hired by the club who would be there waiting for him. Although they earned incomparably less than the star players, these mysterious hooded fellows were charged with roughing them up on these occasions, naturally without hurting them badly since they were worth millions.

The club also used another complementary method. Sam Gere, the assistant coach, was supposed to visit the players' houses at night to check if they were there. He always went armed with a pen and a pad to take note of anything worth noting. The athletes' productivity must not be lessened by youthful reveries.

This character was unbearable and truly scared me. He would go by my home on any day at any time. And like a prison guard he always came back, at least twice a week, sometimes three or four times, always with the same care, with the same face like an inspector, and always dressed in the same training suit, holding the same pen and pad. How many times I went downstairs in my pajamas, yawning and rubbing my eyes, just so that he could get a look at me.

"Yes, I'm home! (I would say as I looked through the peephole of the door). I was already asleep, woke up when the bell rang. Please don't come by so often. Thank you."

"Hi," he said, laughing softly. He looked like a ghost, a ghost with a cynical smile. His weapon was his pad. When he spun on his heels and left, I went back to bed muttering. At least I was sure that my name would not be underlined in red.

One night I managed to get away. I reckoned that Same Gere would not come by that night, and I was right, he didn't. I went out to unwind, and I really needed to. The team had lost a game the weekend before and the press had been biting in its criticism of me. I was so upset that I couldn't sleep. Plus Renata was away. She had been on the catwalk that day and had decided to go out with other models, something that she was unfortunately much given to doing.

I left home full of worries, driving slowly with my lights off. I managed to get past one, two, three blocks. Now nothing could stop me from having fun. I had to take advantage of my good luck. It was like a prison-break. I really needed to loosen up a bit in a bar. It meant a lot to me that day.

I drove for over an hour along a winding road, not at all like the big thoroughfares. The whole way was curves and more curves so that I felt like a formula 1 driver. I had just put on new tires. They clung wonderfully to the road. They were worth the money. And they had cost a lot. No normal person could afford tires like those.

I stopped the car in a parking lot near an out of the way bar, with loud music, where lots of drinking was going on, a real uproar. I got out of the car. I was unrecognizable. I had bought a disguise some time before: long hair, a beard and a yellow jacket. I put it all on as best I could. I also had a broad-rim hat that hid my face.

Nobody recognized me in the bar. The employees and customers walked by me without a second look, as though I were nobody. How wrong they were! There stood Daniel Malka, the famous football player, but very well disguised.

Smiling and happy, I drank a beer, then another and another, munching on peanuts. Then I had a coffee, then another. And then I ordered beer again. I felt great there. What fun! A famous athlete had managed to shake off the informants spread out over the city and evade the assistant coach's deadly notepad.

A stuttering old drunk walked over, sat down and began to talk to me. He reeked of liquor and took forever to get out what he wanted to say.

"Hey there, young man. Mind if... mind if I have a seat here? That's... that's very kind of you. I see you're... you're not from around here. I ain't... I ain't seen you here before. If you were... if you were a regular I'd recognize you. I know th... th... this bar... like... like the palm of my hand. I... I used to be a handsome guy. The g... girls used to like me, used to like me a lot. Th... th... they really liked me. At least... at least so it seemed. I w... w... wasn't anything to s... s... sneeze at. I've b... b... been coming to this bar for thirty years, no, for f... f... forty years. No that's not right. L...lemme think. I w... w... was born in... When was I born? Oh, I know, I know. I was b... b... born in... N... n... now I can't remember."

A waiter walked up with his apron hanging loose and a pen behind his ear and began to ask me what kind of women I liked. I didn't hear him the first time or the second, so he had to repeat every question three times. The reason for this apparent deafness was obvious: that stuttering old drunk was driving me crazy. He wouldn't shut up. I felt like telling him I'd heard enough of his absurd tale, but I didn't say anything. I had to be discreet.

When it was closing time I paid the bill and stumbled out of the bar. I had drunk too much. The old drunk stayed there, singing his own praises. It was cold out, with a light mist. I put on my yellow jacket and headed toward the car. Then I felt someone touch me on the shoulder.

"Taking a walk around here at this time of night?"

It was the well-known TV host Mark Russel, standing next to me. I was stunned by his sudden appearance. And he was not alone. A battalion of reporters and photographers were with him. The Ferrari had been my undoing. Someone had tipped off the press. I was going to pay dear for my little escapade.

I tried to get away as fast as I could. I ducked into the car and started the engine. I turned around and hit the pedal. A bit later I ran over something, but I wasn't sure what at the time. Later I found out it was a stray cat. Reporters, photographers and customers from the bar were all terribly sorry for the poor beast.

A few hours later, around eight in the morning, the TV news led with a report that terrified me.

"Good morning. And now the top of the news. Daniel Malka was involved in a serious traffic accident this morning as he left a local bar. At four a.m. he left the premises dressed like a clown. In the image on your screen you can see him getting into his car, sporting a fake beard and wearing very odd clothes. The accident took place soon afterwards. In his haste to get away from reporters Daniel roared off recklessly in his Ferrari and crushed a cat under his one of his front wheels. The poor animal survived for a few moments, meowing for his life, which however ended moments later, with the light of life still glimmering in its eyes. The reporters and photographers at the scene were greatly moved. The Association for the Protection of Animals has condemned the animal's death at the football player's hands, pointing out that he should be setting a good example for society instead of being a paradigm of cowardly degradation. Everybody is now waiting for a formal response from Daniel and his club. His morning training session is set for ten a.m. Sources close to the organization have told us that Daniel stands to be severely penalized."

In the following days the headlines told the story in outrageous terms, implying that I had gone looking to the bar to find lovers. This caused me serious problems at home: Renata broke a vase on my head.

Things did not go any better at the club. The president broke off a business trip abroad to take care of the matter. He was not at all happy with me. He immediately summoned me to his office for a meeting with him and the coach, openly telling me not to bring Renata. He was truly afraid of her.

I showed up at the appointed hour. The president was livid, his forehead wrinkled. He didn't say hello. The TV in his office was on with the volume turned up very loud. An acrobat was singing as he performed. The crowd was waving hands in the air. There were so many happy people in the world. But I was not one of them.

Suddenly, breaking his controlled immobility, the president spoke to me, thrusting a finger into the air.

"There will be no debate about what happened, Daniel. The proof is in the papers. We will keep half your pay as a fine. The coach will have to penalize you too. I called you in just to give you some advice. Use your youth to dedicate yourself to the game. You are a high-priced horse. You have to sleep at night to be able to spend your days running. Don't subvert that logic. You will have plenty of time to wallow in drink once your career has ended. At that point you can kill yourself if you like. I won't care. But not now. Sleep and run. Just be a good horse."

I was shocked that the coach, who had always been my friend, agreed completely with the president. Nervously chain-smoking he proved even more radical, speaking of my loins.

"Let me tell you, Daniel: I am sick of putting up with young men whose bank accounts are full at the beginning of the month, and by the middle have spent nearly everything, without any respect for the president or me. Don't waste your life. I want to see you galloping. The rhythm of your hooves has to be steady, strong, steadfast. You have to run and run, sweat and sweat, so your loins will gleam like those of a black horse at the end of a race."

As punishment for my nocturnal adventure the coach kept me on the bench. The club lost money and games as a result. The crowd went down by a figure of ten thousand compared to the usual attendance and the team was whipped by three goals to zero, which caused a national scandal and infuriated the fans. They tore chairs out of the stadium and threw them over the protective barriers.

Without my presence at midfield each player tried to win the game by himself. The result was scandalous defeat. They unfolded banners in the stands, demanding that the coach's head roll. The masseur was attacked; the goalkeeper was threatened. They snickered at the president.

From time to time life shows men the real dimension of things and their importance. There are facts that shake the very structure of being, showing us how frail we are. Compared to such facts the texture of a leather ball and the quality of a kick mean nothing.

One morning my maid did not show up. She had been run over, and died. I was extremely upset at this dramatic turn of events. I asked the coach if I could skip a practice session. The answer was an unadorned "No."

"No!" (He said). "I used to be a player too. I was playing when my father died. I was training when my mother died. I went to their funerals but with a very clear idea: First come obligations, then emotions. Let's go train, Gladiator. We have a game on Sunday."

Feelings turned to stone. The blinding will to win hardened the mind. Athletes became machines. They dreamt only of goals, interviews, drugs, women and cheating. So many harsh training sessions caused the athletes serious harm and did not bode well for their old age. It was gilded servitude, but they were slaves nonetheless.

The relationship between athletes, coaches, managers, owners and agents was constantly poisoned by nasty rumors, news reports and players coveting each other's spouses. I was always worried about getting hurt, or getting bad press in the sports news, or about interviews I had to give, or the need to expand my vocabulary to deal with reporters, or about dietary restrictions and the temptation to take too many vitamins.

My life was reduced to training, traveling, being stuck in hotels, and playing, plus advertising duties and photo ops to make more and more money. In my hours of leisure, which were rare indeed, I roared around in my

Ferrari, risking my life, and wrangled with Renata over her excesses. Nothing gave me peace of mind. Nothing was uplifting.

I was always on the road. Squandering my youth. Three times a week I woke up in a room where many people had already breathed the air. They only changed the furniture and the color of the curtains. I traveled from my room to the lobby and from the lobby to my room. My teammates did the same. We had nothing to say to each other except banalities and swear-words.

Sometimes for fun I moved among the reporters, at the entrance to a hotel, with thick books under my arm. It was just for a photo op. As soon as I glanced at a few letters I became confused. I tried to make some headway, five pages at a time, until I felt exhausted and finally picked up a sports newspaper. If I picked up the wrong one my brain would begin to simmer again. The topics in fashion were PSI20, balancing the budget, the Bad Bank and interest rates, all of them topics for a wiser man than me.

Idiotic conversations and computer games – on the road there was nothing else to cultivate the soul or lift the spirit. What mattered to the club was that the players knew how to take good shots on goal. Nobody taught us how to speak carefully and well, to say things that mattered, in a measured rhythm, not too fast and not too slow, using the volume of the voice to tonal advantage, articulating correctly, without making bestial noises.

It was in a play with my teammate Foxman during a practice session that I strained my leg and felt a crack in my left knee. I didn't at once understand how serious it was. But it was a torn ligament. This was the first major setback of my career. Two days later I had to be operated on.

The post-operative shock was awful. I felt unbearable pain. And solitude, too. I was alone in my room. The limelight of the press had vanished. For months I had to work out by myself with the physiotherapist in charge of my physical and psychological recovery. Finally I was able to rejoin the team and use a ball, so that I could recharge my body and not go around always feeling sorry for myself. The press only remembered that I existed when I was fully recovered. Until then I was a zombie.

Other serious injuries followed. I tore the cartilage in both my knees and had to live with that for the rest of my career until those wounds put an end to it. I had difficulty squatting, I could not use my limbs with the same freedom: they would crack. I was constantly subject to excess liquid in my knees and little by little that aggravated my clinical state.

At every turn, it seemed, the club doctor would show up to give me an injection.

"Come on, Daniel, it's just a little shot."

When I walked into room 12 of the hospital for the last time, to have yet another operation, I felt completely frustrated. I was not afraid of the operation itself, which was performed by competent surgeons under general anesthesia. What I feared was the physical suffering and the painful recovery that faced me on waking from surgery. I had been through that four times already. And this time I would not have the strength to go through the same process once more. I was prostrate. I would never play again.

And so my career, so full of success, of awards and personal triumphs, interviews and photo ops, came to an end. Sadly, it had been cut short by the torture of injuries, operations and long periods of inactivity.

The club was not held hostage to my reputation for very long. Soon another exceptional young player emerged from the underworld, as I had in my day. He had a contagious talent and enormous physical strength. After a month the fans had forgotten me. It was the end. My time was over.

I t was because I was so dazed by my desire for greatness and stardom that I broke off my engagement with Miriam, a simple girl wholly devoid of such ambitions, and married Renata Bianchi, professional model. This event was played up by the press and TV as a great social occasion.

Miriam was so traumatized by the news that she had to be hospitalized, overcome as she was by a sudden psychiatric illness. At first she dressed in garbs of mourning, saying that I had died in an airplane crash.

A few months later she began to nourish the illusion that my body would never be recovered, so that I might still be alive and return at any time. She doffed her widow's garments and sat at the window every day hoping to see the man she loved appear on our street.

The neighbors crowded the sidewalk to see the poor creature sitting at the window, no longer speaking of workers' rights and equality between men and women, but living out a drama of love. She nodded sweetly to everyone, saying she was waiting for me and that I would come back, since once upon a time I had promised I would return and marry her. I wasn't just part of her life. I was her life.

One day, thinking she saw my silhouette in the mist, Miriam was so deeply moved that her heart failed her. A few hours later she was pronounced dead. A life lost, a hope destroyed, a beautiful voice silenced forever, to the sorrow of those who were close to her and (as she herself would say) of the multitude of underprivileged workers.

Willy-nilly I was the cause of her death. I spent some horrible weeks. I suffered like a dog. So, feeling that I had to tell someone, I told Renata what had happened. She crossed her legs, revealing her new stockings, spoke to me of a new perfume and changed the TV channel, humming. It was a shocking lack of sensitivity.

I proposed to Renata without knowing what her feelings were, unconcerned if she was a serious person. A few weeks after our wedding I was so unhappy I cried. All the hopes I had entertained during our engagement were dashed. For her, marriage was not a matter of the heart. It was just a commercial contract. She did not get married to have a home (which she didn't want) or children (which she couldn't have for health reasons) but to enjoy the material benefits and an unfettered freedom to cultivate all her vices, including nights-in-a-row out with merry groups of friends, seated at the tables of the worst dives, crossing her legs like a loose woman and staying there from evening until dawn, laughing, drinking and smoking in suspect ease with professional spend-thrifts.

Renata's professional life was quite ridiculous. The tools of her trade were her body and a special skill in thrusting her butt into the air. She would change her outfit twenty times a day, constantly worried about her appearance.

The public knew her by her expensive clothes, parties, trips, reputation, and naked body. These were all aspects of her profession. But there were others: a strict diet, physical and psychological suffering, and shrieks of rebellion. She was 5'10" and weighed 135 pounds. If she got any heavier she would become hysterical, and in her madness went on a radical diet, taking prescription drugs and laxatives, working out at the gym all day long and eating just two peanuts and a lettuce leaf for dinner. That kind of work is nothing to boast about.

She had black hair that would be blown about by the slightest breeze. This was a calculating and haughty woman whose behavior in every situation bespoke a sense of her own superiority in relation to all other beings.

One day she decided, irate, that she would go to the team's locker-room. But she couldn't because the security man at the door to the tunnel at the stadium took his job very seriously.

"Excuse me, Ma'am, but you can't go through here. This is a restricted area."

"I am Daniel Malka's wife", Renata said. "I can go by here all right. And I am going in. If you don't mind..."

"I'm sorry" (said the security man, laying his hand on Renata's shoulder). "Only players, coaches and members of the board can enter. Nobody else gets through this door."

"Do you know who I am, you brute? I am the famous model Renata Bianchi! I've won hundreds of prizes, contests, medals and honors!"

"Yes, and do you know who I am? I am Tommy" (said the security man, leaving Renata in a state of incomprehension.

"You are nobody! Is the Vice-President here?" (Renata insisted.)

"Possibly. You will have to go to Reception and ask. It's on the other side of the stadium."

"You're the one that has to go to Reception, not me."

"Could you please get out of the way? I am going to close the door (said the security man, gently pushing Renata back."

"Call the Vice-President or you'll be out of a job. Now!"

"If you don't mind…"

And whack! The door shut. Renata's threats were a total bluff. She had this obsession about threatening everybody. The security man was not going to be fired for doing his job. But the scene gives you a good idea of the overbearing character of the woman I chose as a wife. A plague. Her teeth scraped on her words and wounded the air, like fingernails scratching a blackboard.

Renata was a beautiful woman, very beautiful. Her curves bewitched experts in fashion and kings of the catwalk. She dressed sumptuously. Often, fearing that nobody appreciated the expensive dress she had bought the day before, she would toss it aside and go looking for another that could attract attention by its novelty.

That plague even made me her cook. At the stadium I was master of the ball; in house I was master of the stove, a kind of deluxe houseboy. She would eat dinner, drink her coffee and rush out of the house. With her cigarette burning away in the corner of her mouth, she'd slam the door on her way out. She was brazen in everything. A woman forever obsessed with her trimmings, hopping about (and dripping with makeup) from one show to another without being in the least satisfied by any of them.

I soon understood the extent of my wife's duplicity and only stuck to the marriage as a question of convenience. The press never talked about Renata without mentioning my name and never talked about me without mentioning hers. Our names were always linked. They were nearly a single name, like a business or a brand. Our marriage was a professional obligation. And a divorce would mean throwing away bags of money.

How often we left home side by side with smiles on our lips, like a happy family, for the sake of appearances on TV and in shots taken by wandering photographers. At other times we would throw open the doors of our home for gossip magazines, whose readers loved catching a glimpse of the love-life of princes and princesses, with their sentimental liaisons, dramas and betrayals.

While I was a professional football player I heard many conversations about investments. In the team locker-room there was a lot of talk about bad investments with stories of players who had once been rich and famous but had fallen into poverty. All my teammates thought like I did.

I still remember our conversations in the locker-room. We seemed like clocks tolling the same hour over and over. "You have to be careful when you invest!" "A lot of former players are living in poverty!" "They won't get me!" "My wife was right: you have to be careful!"

Shame on all of us! We could not understand that all investments are bad and no business works unless the businessman in charge of things is for real. That was what Jason taught me one day, neatly and clearly.

"Daniel, when your career ends there will only be one line of work for you: not to spend money. As a business man you will always be a zero."

Nothing could be truer. My calling was to be a midfielder, to take shots on goal, to control the ball with my chest and bring it gracefully to the goal line. I was good on attack, better on defense. As to business... my God! I was a complete disaster at creating wealth and dealing with sums of money.

My existence was full of training sessions, road-trips and advertising gigs. I never had the time or peace of mind to think about any business deals that might appear. I said yes to everything. The few times that I said no it was a mistake. An absolute disaster. I had no business sense at all.

As soon as I married Renata, members of her family began to tear each other's flesh like hungry wolves, pretending they wanted to help me handle my money and make good investments in real estate and clothing. I tried to please all of them and so contribute to family harmony. They soon began to wear tuxedoes and dress shoes as they spent my money in casinos. They identified themselves as agents of the businessman and football player Daniel Malka.

There were countless business meetings scheduled for the morning that they could not miss if they were going to represent me. But after long nights of whisky and cigars… it was so good to stay in bed. So they missed crucial meetings that they had set up with buyers or sellers, and more of my money went down the tube. Other times they showed up on time. But then the deals were a disaster, so it would have been better if they had not showed up at all.

One day Renata spoke to me all in a tizzy.

"I was thinking, Daniel. You're always bringing home medals. We have no place to put them all. Same thing with my old clothes, my shoes, and clippings from the interviews I've given for all these years."

"What do you suggest?" (I asked.)

"Well, I've given it a lot of thought. I've decided we should create a museum with two rooms, one dedicated to you and the other to me. We'll call it the Daniel and Renata Museum."

"I don't much like that idea. There's nothing more

ridiculous than self-praise. For me and for you. As far as me, I'd rather do something for the street I grew up in. I'm not sure what. Maybe build a home for orphans; maybe a welfare center for older folks that don't have enough to eat; maybe repairs for the school; or perhaps donate a wing to the hospital; something like that."

"You are so dumb, Daniel." she said. "You don't understand anything about anything. We'll create a museum. I've already given orders to begin. The museum will be on Main Street in town. I know the right spot. It's very expensive but it's worth it."

"Are you sure it will be a good deal?"

"Absolutely. We will also invest in a hotel in the building right next to it. It will be the first hotel in chain to be called "Gladiator and Renata." We'll spread these hotels across the globe. I've already told the bank to transfer our accounts – the ones that make money – to this project. My cousin is taking care of everything. She has a degree in marketing."

"What? I don't believe it.", I said. "That is a lot of money. It's everything we have so far. Are you sure that...?"

"No problem!" she said. "It's a sure thing. If need be the banks can help us finance the project."

"Jason says that if it's a good idea you don't need to ask for a bank loan."

At this Renata bristled and lost her cool. She would become furious and foam with rage whenever anyone questioned her caprices. And if that anyone was Jason...

"Jason is an idiot (she said). He's got a mind the size

of a pea, soaked in scotch and tobacco. A real mediocrity. He doesn't understand anything about anything. This is going to be a real triumph. My cousin..."

"When my career is over, the "Gladiator" brand may not be worth anything. That's what Jason says. Maybe he's right."

"Don't you dare speak to me about that thug. Trust me. I told you: my cousin has a degree in marketing. With honors. Next to her Jason is a midget."

The hotel deal was a total failure. The construction ended halfway through. It ended when I found out that the project couldn't get a permit. Renata's cousin, although she had a degree, was completely irresponsible and incompetent. I had to sell the building while it was still being built so I didn't lose everything I had invested. The project to create a world-wide chain of hotels with the "Gladiator and Renata" brand obviously only existed on paper. No bank would back Renata's crazy idea.

The museum was created. It cost a fortune to buy the building and modernize it. And the original budget was left far behind. I ended up owing the bank a gigantic sum. Then, a few days before it was inaugurated, the museum was destroyed in a fire. Renata's cousin had left a burning candle inside. Worse still, she had forgotten to insure the place. I lost everything.

That day I cried on the shoulder of my best friend, Mark. He owned a jewelry store in the center of the city. He never asked to borrow money from me and warned me to be careful of self-interested opportunists and false friends. He gave me good advice.

Our conversations were almost always about football or Renata's nasty personality. It seemed a true friendship, one that increased my happiness and eased my frustration. Sometimes we would eat in an upscale restaurant. He would bring Rose and insist that I bring Renata. There was a warm atmosphere. Rose, who was a charming girl, would speak softly and slowly. She wore such dazzling jewels that my wife would go crazy and buy them all from her, piece by piece. Often enough Rose would arrive decked out with jewelry and by the middle of lunch only retained her clothes. It was me that wrote the checks.

Sadly, I learned later on that Mark used Rose like a human showcase. The people he invited to lunch were no more than theater props intended to stir Renata up so he could sell her the most expensive jewelry he had, at double the price.

Before we had lunch Rose would stop by the jewelry shop and trim herself out with gems, and afterwards, if she didn't sell them to Renata, she would stop by the shop again and put the jewels back in the showcase. She usually didn't have anything to put back though. And Mark would tell his acquaintances that I was a "sucker duck", and even blurt out "Quack, quack, quack!"

While I was a football player I didn't live only one expensive life. I lived various very expensive lives: my own, that of Renata, and those of her family and false friends. All of them lived as though my supply of money would never end. All of them thought they had the right to enjoy the same kind of life I led.

Just the fancy cars, all paid for by me, that they all had in their garages were worth more than I would have needed to spend the rest of my life without working. Add to this the fact that they all purchased new cars twice a year, spending large sums each time. In the ten years of my career the total expense was more than many millions. Just in cars. That's without counting dozens of other equally expensive excesses.

When the football seasons ended and vacation time began, I would be completely reborn. I wanted to fill my suitcases and go to another continent, to spend a month staying out all night, getting drunk, eating feasts and gambling in casinos. Renata's family and other friends would always go with me.

My motto was "splurge" before the new season began and with it another year shut inside hotels and chasing down a ball. Their motto was the same as mine, even though they produced nothing in their own lives. We bought everything we felt like buying, at any price: amusements, boats, cars, drinks, big meals, everything we could think of. The holidays ended quickly. Work started again. The games began.

I will never forget the day that Renata convinced me to pay the whole price tag for her sister's wedding and throw a party with silver table settings. A wedding worth a million. One thousand guests, five photographers, the best musicians. The bride's gown cost a huge wad. So did the bridegroom's clothes. For her hairdo and makeup the bride hired a foreign company. Among other things they sent three professionals who stayed with her the whole day long. The happy couple drove off in a limousine fifteen meters long. Their honeymoon was a trip around the world. And there was much more extravagance.

I arrived early at the church where the wedding was to be held. I found a big parking space for the Ferrari, although there was someone working the area to aid those wishing to park cars, and he insisted on guiding me into the spot. He did this with his right hand while his left hovered near my window in search of a tip.

At first he asked me for money for his addiction. Then, when I refused, he tried to bum a cigarette. I told him I didn't smoke but he didn't believe me. For several minutes, with his nearly toothless mouth contorted in resentment, he accused me of lying. Finally he spun halfway around on his heels, muttering in anger. I thought he might try to get back at me by scratching the doors or slashing the tires.

At the church-door there was a tense moment. The wedding guests were tightly packed there, an enormous swath of people. John, the bridegroom's father, seemed to preside over this impressive assembly, awakening the attention of the photographers. With a megaphone in his right hand he proudly affirmed that the newlyweds would be the happiest couple in the world. He only let go of the megaphone and lowered the volume of his voice when a frightening scream echoed around.

It was the bridegroom, who had just arrived, his head stuck out the window, greeting all those present. Next to him was someone with an accordion playing away on his instrument. The bridegroom was about to realize his highest dream: to marry someone. His second most important dream was to fill that someone with children, and so make sure that so fine a lineage as his would not come to an end.

The bride came soon after, in an American limousine that I rented at a very high price. He arrived sobbing, which I thought very strange, but I did not immediately try to find out why.

"Hoorah!" (Renata shouted when she saw her sister arrive.)

After greeting the guests the bride went into the church, followed by four candelabras. I did not attend the religious ceremony. I didn't even go into the church. I remained seated calmly on an esplanade.

I remember that when the ceremony had ended the bridegroom quickly lifted up his bride and got into the limousine, which at once sped off towards the restaurant. Dozens of footballs were tied to the tailpipe -- another of Renata's ideas.

The limousine had hardly gone a few blocks when it stopped working. The bride, bothered because the car was making a lot of noise, had decided to stuff a cloth into the exhaust pipe. The damage was serious and I would pay for it. The happy couple found another means of transportation and continued on their way, unperturbed.

Worried about the high cost of all that, and very upset with my family life, I went to the parking lot to get my Ferrari. As soon as I got close to the car I had a tremendous shock: the paintjob had been scratched by a knife.

Far away, atop some buildings, someone was laughing and gloating. It was the man who worked in the parking lot and who like a stray cat glided from one rooftop to another. I called the police, but it did no good. The fellow faded from sight. I went my way, my cheeks flushed in anger.

After half an hour, inside the restaurant where the wedding feast had taken place, the owner came up to me and identified himself, his face glowing. His name was Jeff and he had scraped through life by buying and selling washing machines. I looked at him cautiously. He was wearing a light blue suit and a loud red tie. His levity seemed to be written across his restless appearance.

The times were long in the past when I used to go hungry on my old street. That day I was feeding a thousand people. All of them could order seven dishes. There were footballs on the tables. It was an outrageous waste of food and footballs. And nobody could dine in peace because John spent the whole time telling senseless anecdotes over a loudspeaker.

Meanwhile, at the main table rumors were taking over. After trading a few secrets the newlyweds began to talk to me and asked about their wedding present, which they had not yet received. Blinded by their ingratitude I pointed my inexorable index finger at them both and blurted out in sheer rage.

"That's enough!"

They exploded in insults and threats and I stopped protesting. I think I went back on the offensive a bit later, but was restrained by Renata who stomped on my foot under the table.

During the fifth course the lights went out for some unknown reason. A waiter walked over to the electric switches, to see correct the problem. But as soon as he touched a switch he got a terrific shock and fell down on the floor.

At this point a bottle of white wine flew through the air and landed at the feet of a shabbily dressed young woman. The poor girl, visibly injured, began to stumble forward. Two groups of people started accusing each other of having thrown the bottle. All this turned into one vast fistfight with an avalanche of punches and kicks every which-way.

In the middle of that cacophony of strident screams an odd figure appeared: the man who had vandalized my car in the lot near the church. Taking advantage of the general panic and unable to restrain his greed, he went into action. He looked around, began to stuff dozens of silver utensils into his pockets, and then found what he really wanted: the closet where they ladies' purses and handbags were stored.

To ward off this imminent robbery I tried to intercept him. I drew near him very carefully (not wanting to have a knife stuck in my heart) and asked him to rethink his idea. But the clever fellow, fully engaged in his activities, gave me a threatening look, gathered up some more purses, and leaped through a window.

There was no time to breathe. Suddenly the curtains caught fire. The flames began to spread. The smoke was suffocating. In a matter of minutes the restaurant became one enormous conflagration. The guests, a thousand of them, abandoned the place in chaos, amid overturned chairs and shattered plates.

While the sun on the horizon cast its last rays of daylight, near the restaurant there was a feverish turmoil. Some lives were still in danger in the fire inside. Two imposing firetrucks and a police car arrived at the scene of the tragedy, with sirens blaring and enormous fanfare.

I heard a horn that seemed like a bomb. It came from an enormous red car, a large typically American vehicle with horns on the hood, phosphorescent stickers on the windows and boxing gloves hanging from the rearview mirror. The door opened and a vaguely familiar character emerged.

John, the bride's father, turned to me irate, accusing me of not having given the couple a gift. I lost my head. I grabbed him by the collar, pounded his pathetic face and then, when he was lying flat on the ground, reminded him that I had paid for the whole wedding, the church, the feast, the clothes, the limousine, the myriad lights, the honeymoon and even a hundred footballs. I only stopped screaming when with his right hand he signaled surrender.

When my career ended I immediately stopped receiving a princely salary from the club and the money from advertising contracts which I had become used to. The mountain of money which I had been getting every month was abruptly replaced by a handful of nothing. And yet the bills I had to pay kept on arriving at the same tempo as always – a terrifying tempo, since my circumstances had been turned upside down.

Renata lost no time at all. She initiated divorce proceedings, demanding fifty percent of the money, goods and property that we had in common. At first I vigorously refused, but she went forward with her plan, blackmailing me with the threat of a scandal in the newspapers. That was what became of my romantic moment a few years before. That was what I got for having trusted her with some secrets of my youth. Her mother, her sister, and her brother-in-law knew those secrets too.

Renata cleverly tricked and intimidated me with threats and I couldn't even react to the false reports that she placed in the newspapers with completely shameless headlines like "Daniel Accused of Striking Renata!!" or "Renata Cries In Agony!" or "This Good Woman Lives In Torture!" or "Daniel's Cruelty."

She even lied in an interview on TV, railing about me. The program was called "I Was a Victim of Domestic Violence." The interviewer was moved by Renata's verbal performance and got her to go into details. She recounted private matters mixed with brazen lies. The next day a poll showed that 97% of those questioned believed Renata's allegations.

An unexpected tax bill on top of the sudden loss of income and the incredibly expensive divorce just added to the disaster. It was a fatal combination, a perfect storm. I had to sell the few assets I still possessed. I was completely ruined: I had no money, no home, no car, no job. I was so badly off that I had to go to the home of friends to be able to eat.

The press quickly came crashing down on top of me. The same newspapers that had once sold whole editions thanks to my success were now sporting banner headlines about my catastrophes. The jackals tore into the carcass. "Daniel Sells His Ferrari!" "Daniel Can't Pay His Taxes!" "Daniel Homeless!" "Poverty Hits Daniel!" "Ruined: Daniel And His Wife!" "Daniel Returns To Parents' Home!" "Daniel Didn't Listen To His Wife!" "Daniel Brought Down By Vanity And Lust!"

I was finally drinking fame's poison, after basking for so many years in the limelight of the press, from cover to cover, seeing only smiles and interviews. The public that had once applauded me now gorged itself on my tragic fate, buying up the newspapers, which often sold out, and delighting in my rotten luck. A world without a soul. A world of ice where I slipped while moving at top speed and fell into the abyss.

Media stardom contains within itself the seeds of its own destruction. I can bear witness to that. It generates envy that can lay low anyone it makes famous. Mediocre people, full of rancor and frustrated with their own lives, really enjoy seeing stars fall at the feet of society.

Downtown I was mistreated many times by common citizens who felt a kind of ecstasy at my disgrace. One individual, his brow wrinkled, walked up, stuck his nose in my face, and said spluttering:

"Hey, Daniel! So the good life is over! Get a job, you bum! You used to race around in a Ferrari with a blond model next to you. And me on foot, without work, in this society that only promotes mediocre folks like you. Now your money's gone and it's your turn to suffer."

"Why do you talk to me like that, sir? (I asked him, taken aback.) I made mistakes in my private life. Lots of mistakes. I trusted the wrong people. That's true. I acted as though money were endless. That's right. But I gave a lot to charity, I always greeted my fans, I never hurt other players, I didn't trade the club I loved for some other more lucrative contract. Now I'm paying for my mistakes by being poor. That's enough. I don't think it's fair for you to badmouth me."

"Shut up, Daniel. Not another word out of you! I have a mind to sock that stupid face of yours."

"Excuse me, sir, but this conversation is over (I said). I was born among thieves. I was educated by street fights. If you push me, I might get angry and break a few of your bones. But I'd rather not do that. Take care. Goodbye."

This sad and humiliating scene made me remember the story of the snake and the firefly, which Baba Madri had told me. The firefly was inoffensive and friendly and wasn't part of the snake's food chain. In life it had glimmered, and that was enough for the snake to want it dead.

After the deadly news that targeted me came a sepulchral and devastating silence, as if Daniel Malka had never trodden the turf of a football stadium, as if he had never existed. The "Gladiator" disappeared from society's consciousness. Now I had to confront a wholly new sensation: the harshness of being totally forgotten.

The Professional Football Players' Association quickly set up a public solidarity fund, giving its bank account number and asking for help of any amount, great or small, from any kind soul who might be moved by the lamentable life I was living. And the message was moving: "Daniel Malka began with nothing. He earned everything by blood, sweat and tears. He won many championships for his club and for the national team. Unexpected misfortune ruined his life."

Nobody believed in the idea of unexpected misfortune. Such misfortune was fully to be expected. In that sense, and despite all the publicity that went with the Association's initiative, the amount they managed to raise was absolutely laughable. It wasn't even enough to pay my last round of debts.

And then... as though I were carrying the weight of the world on my shoulders, I went back, desolate, with head bowed, to the street where I was born and grew up, a world of suffering and poverty, without bread, without a roof, and without health.

I got a ride from a friend who owned a van. I took with me a suitcase of clothes, some bedroom furniture, a small kit with a toothbrush and things like that, and a watch. Nothing else. It was cold. Around my neck I wore a Ferrari scarf that I had bought once upon a time to drive my car with the top down. How amazing, how incredible life is! How it changes. More quickly than the day. More quickly than the night.

Silent, sad and old, my father opened the front door. Time had passed. Wrinkles now covered his face. He limped and used a cane. His eyeglasses were as thick as the glass at the bottom of a bottle. During my time as a football star I had done little to help him. Now I had a heavy conscience. This poor man who brought me up, gave me my first lessons and believed in me had during years followed my games with a hand-held radio.

While my father settled in on the sofa, his head hung over his knees, my mother walked into the room and came over to me crying.

"What happened, darling? What happened? How did you spend so much money? Ten years ago your father and I thought we would never have to worry about you again. We thought your future was guaranteed. And it turns out…"

"…that I spent everything", I said.

"And what happened to Renata, son? Why didn't she ever want to meet us?"

"That woman is a viper that came into my life to bite me and hurt me. I would rather not talk about her. I'm just very sorry."

I quickly took my suitcase and furniture to my room, my eyes lowered. I was crushed by shame. My mother stood there looking at me with her arms spread wide, as if she were asking the heavens to explain the unexplainable. Poor thing! I adored my poor mother. Her life had not changed much since my departure. Her lot was to suffer in gloom from sun-up to sundown, cleaning every corner of the house, hoping for better days which now might never come.

I sat propped at the window, my eyes fixed on the street. I had spent a decade proudly surveying the most beautiful scenes that money can buy, and now a simple look at my street sent shivers through me. That view of the sky with clothes hung out to dry, forever dripping, and the jungle of concrete colored with graffiti seemed to my stunned eyes a frightful scenario.

From that same window where long before I had watched, euphoric, as Jason signaled to me, I now saw shabby boys hurling tin cans at one another. I had been like that too. Those kids were getting to know many dangers, but there were many other dangers that they could not even imagine, or didn't understand were dangers, until they were enmeshed and trapped in them.

Those days, weeks and months were painful. I spent my time at the window, or walking up and down the street, with no direction or aim. It was the life of someone without money, without a job, someone who feels ashamed to show his face in front of others, someone who had gotten rich and then become poor again, squandering his money or letting others waste it lavishly and scandalously on fine things.

The old football field no longer existed. That ancient warehouse had been torn down and the spot was now a garbage heap where all kinds of things were dumped -- garbage from drugs, or domestic and industrial waste.

It was a sign of the times. Even in housing developments kids tend to stop playing football.

The street was no longer the one I had known. It had gotten worse. When it was hot, after dinner the residents would come out of their buildings and sit on the sidewalk, hiding their joyless faces like a defeated army. They always talked about the same things: beggars, desolation, crime, death. Now there was a new topic: the rise and fall of a football player from that street. His name was Daniel Malka.

Men with suits and ties sometimes visited the street to examine the living conditions. They spoke for the government, or for the political parties, or for social security. Usually they were chased out with stones if they would not promise to arrange subsidies for everyone. The people who lived there didn't believe in generic promises since they always turned out to be hollow.

Prostitutes danced on the sidewalks trying to attract clients. In the doorways of the buildings the pimps lingered, checking how much money they were taking in. Those women had a sad destiny. Sometimes their competition for a good locale would degenerate into knife fights. And it did them no good to wait in dark places. A lamp was worth its weight in gold. They knew that. So did the undertaker.

I had known the undertaker since I was a child. He was glum, never seemed to like his work. Coffins came and went in the grim cave where he lived. He wore a grey wrinkled suit and did not laugh or speak or show emotion. He just carried the coffins in a van and buried them on the north side of the street's overcrowded cemetery, which was a kind of mass grave.

The number of beggars was multiplying at an alarming rate. Like the prostitutes, the beggars could only be seen until around two o'clock in the morning. After that hour the night belonged to the dogs. There were hundreds of them. They barked and growled and bit the passers-by. They lived off sacks of garbage full of the remains of food that the neighbors had thrown out of the windows of their apartments during the day.

The few people who had savings stashed away feared that robbers might break in and kill them to get their money. One of my mother's friends, who during her entire life had been stuffing coins into a sack, locked herself inside her home. The coins she possessed were not money to her; they were life and death.

Except for the humble, who were few, when the people on that street saw that woman who had saved money for her old age, they were filled with envy and loathing. They had no idea what kind of hell she had lived through. She never left home. She slept like a watch-dog with one vigilant eye always open.

One day this poor woman was roughed up and robbed by someone wearing a hood. It was thought that the culprit was a well-known thief who lived on the street. The members of a gang called "The Avengers," who covered their faces when they went into action, decided to go after the robber and break his bones with a sledge-hammer.

They found him drinking a glass of cheap champagne in a cabaret. One Avenger walked up and smashed his head with two resounding blows. Wounded and terrified, the thief ran across the table tops, slipped into the bathroom and locked the door. But a dozen gang members went after him in a ferocious fury and broke down the door with their shoulders.

His situation was critical. Though he had run many risks in his life, nothing could save him now. Still, a bald man in his fifties, who was inspired by peace conferences and diplomatic treaties which were on the rise in the civilized world, strode resolutely to the center of the room with a stick in his hand. This courageous act distracted The Avengers, who approached him, puzzled by this odd character. The thief seized his opportunity and fled, crawling through people's legs and murmuring an unintelligible lament.

Beating his stick on the table, the bald man wanted to offer a narrative criticizing The Avengers. But he was quickly overtaken by punches and head-butts and soon was begging to be forgiven for his thoughtlessness. Those scenes out of movies where the hero overcomes all the bad guys, leaping, kicking and lashing out in every direction, had no place on my street. There the brave made their exit in a coffin.

Grave events were about to occur at the door of the cabaret, where one of The Avengers was standing guard. He suddenly felt someone breathing heavily down his neck – a bad sign. Armed men appeared on all sides. A rival gang wanted to take revenge for a fight they had lost to The Avengers some time before. This violence drew a prompt response. Sounds of a gunfight suddenly rang out. One by one The Avengers' legs crumpled under their enemies' onslaught and they limped off in a chaotic retreat, swearing vengeance.

A month after these events the tit-for-tat had not ended. In fact it had infected other gangs. Brutality spread like hotcakes. Machine-gun fire crackled through the night as violence begot violence, like fire which once lit keeps on flaring up and gaining strength as it moves.

have just rung the doorbell twice at the home of Baba Madri, that solitary old man with no wife, no friends, no job, no human companionship, who lives in his little castle without electricity, a voluntary prisoner. He may be a hundred years old.

My umbrella bends and twists with gusts of wind but still holds out. It's old. It belonged to my paternal grandfather. I feel anguished and insecure. My cheeks are pale. I don't know what I will find. I don't even know if the old master is still alive.

A blinding flash of lightening rips through the sky, foretelling a thunderbolt that booms and reverberates. In the street, under the lamps that remain, the prostitutes struggle to stay on their feet despite the force of wind and rain. The pimps don't let them take shelter. They keep watch from the entries of the buildings, cleaning their nails with knives. They want to get the most out of the activities they exploit. A nightmare scenario. It's not the end of the world, but it might as well be.

At Madri's house nobody answers. Nothing seems to move. Life appears to be extinguished by the death of this old man. I feel remorse. I feel sorry. I remember his face, his posture, his advice. A tear falls. I am about to give up. I hesitate, then decide to leave, disheartened.

But I don't leave. Suddenly the door swings wide open revealing a tall ghostly silhouette. A finger points at my face. Two large eyes are staring at me. My jaw drops in astonishment at this unexpected apparition.

"When Abraham said, 'God brings the light from the East; you must bring it from the West,' the infidel was confused. Of course! God doesn't shepherd the unjust" (Madri said simply).

"Old master (I said, recovering my breath), God forgive me. I am wretched. I feel ill, very ill. Every day I wake up with sharp pains in my head and heart. I feel like I'm going to explode at any moment. It might be my nerves or high blood pressure, or a problem with my eyes. It could be many things. Or several things together."

"Conclusion: you're not ill at all", Madri said. "I know what's weighing on your spirit. You got rich quickly and then quickly got poor. It's well known that an abundance of riches confuses and tortures the spirit, creates a longing for more and more wealth, and makes people lose any sense of what it is to earn and enjoy things. Joseph taught the Egyptians to save up during the years of plenty so they could survive during the years of famine."

"So you know my life? Well... I'm amazed. Yes, it's all true. During the last ten years I got rich playing football. I became famous. My face was known around the globe. I lost all sense of reality. I lived amidst luxury of every kind, bought the best cars, the best jewels, the best clothes, and..."

"And did you feel good living like that?" Madri asked. "I'll confess you, I already know the answer."

"I was always unhappy. And what hurts more than the loss of my money is that I lost Miriam. She got ill and died because of me. I traded her for a beautiful but stupid woman. And I'm so sorry for that."

"One day a fox found a lovely mask and said to it: 'You are very beautiful. But you have no brain.'"

Contrite because I had never gone to visit this old sage when I was rich, I felt deeply repentant and full of good will.

"I would like so much to play again and make money. I would give lots of it to you."

"I wouldn't take it.", he said. "I don't need it. I have everything I need."

"But I see that you live in a very simple home. There's not even any furniture. Where do you keep your things?" (I asked)

"I don't see your furniture either" (replied Baba Madri).

"Mine?" (I said, surprised) "I'm just passing through."

"And I am just passing through this life too", Baba Madri said.

That old man didn't seem to get any older. He seemed sharper and more sure of himself than ever. I looked at him with admiration. He was so different from all the other men I had met in my life. I went on lamenting my plight at great length.

"I lost Miriam and it was my fault. Might she be listening to me in some part of the universe? Does she know how sorry I am?"

"She's very near you. She's with you. Nothing in nature dies. Everything is transformed. That's how it is in the material world. And also in the world of spiritual energy. Human beings are atomically eternal."

"I need to strengthen my knees so I can play football for a few more years. I have to earn money again."

Madri gazed at me and scratched his head under his turban.

"What do you intend to do for the world?" (he asked me)

"For the world? Nothing. I just want to be happy" (I replied).

"Nobody has ever been happy if they don't help others. What time did you get up today? What have you done for the society you live in?"

"Me... nothing" (I stammered).

"I think you are not a stone. These walls, like rocks in space, have no life of their own, no personality or thought. And they never will. They can exist for millions of years but they will never live or think or have an 'I.' But human beings are alive. You, Daniel, are alive. At the beginning of time a Creator created everything. Imagine a bee, a seagull, a dog, a man. The seagull is more intelligent than the bee; the dog is more intelligent than the seagull; man is more intelligent than the dog. There is an increasing degree of creative intelligence and its highest point is the intelligence of the Supreme Creator. Be at peace with God. Climb to the highest point of a city and contemplate the panorama: the logic that surrounds the universe, the laws of nature, astrological truths, life itself, the beauty of nature, the purity of animals. The entire creative Logos will show you the specific mission of your soul."

"What happens if I don't fulfill that mission?" (I asked)

"Your soul will need to be reborn."

"Will I be reborn as another person?"

"Souls, when they are reborn, do not always return as human beings. If after the chances of self-perfection that are offered to it, a soul does not attain the expected righteousness it will become an isolated wanderer in this world until it is reborn in the realm of animals, or vegetables or minerals, or even in the realm of negative spiritual beings. In such cases it is only after a long and difficult period of time that it will again be reborn as a human being."

"I am sure my future will be one of temporary truces and shame", I said. "I have dreamed about that many times."

"You think you're a prophet?" Madri asked.

"No, not at all."

"So don't pay any attention to your silly dreams. They just reflect your thoughts and anxieties. At night you dream about what you are thinking during the day."

"I took a big fall, master. A very big fall. I feel hurt, really hurt."

"It's good for a man to take a fall, so long as it doesn't completely crush him. You must begin to struggle again. Don't always think about your misfortune or it will end up hypnotizing you. You won't be able to act at all."

"I should think positive, is that it?"

"Naturally. And to think positive means just that: to think positive. It does not mean 'Not to think.' Now go."

On the same day that I visited Baba Madri, I began to train. Friends and acquaintances on the street at once encouraged me and some even said they would run with me during the night to protect me from thugs and from shame. Every night I would slip out of the apartment and run through the center of the city. I stretched and did special exercises for my knees. Soon I began to practice with a ball, accompanied by an old unemployed ex-coach whom (luckily) I had met somewhere along the way.

When I no longer felt my knees popping I began to think of a name, which hit me the force of a wave: Jason Parker, the agent who had given me my days of glory – and of money. Our relationship had cooled a long time ago, thanks to Renata's tantrums. In fact, I had lost countless friendships of all kinds thanks to my ex-wife's offensive and aggressive personality.

Jason was worth waiting for, and I waited for four hours in the rain at the door of his elegant home. He arrived in style, driving a sports car with four headlights. Festive music was blasting at full volume from inside the house.

I walked slowly up to the door. My teary eyes told the whole story. I needed help. I was twenty-eight years old. I was still strong, I still had character. With mature talent and technique I still had something to give to football.

Jason turned down the radio and opened the door. He seemed cordial and well disposed towards me.

"Daniel, boy have I missed you! Aren't you going to give me a hug? I hope you're not here to borrow money. I don't lend any to anyone. The most I can do is give you a little, very little, because I work hard to earn it. But no loans. 'For loan oft loses both itself and friend.'"

"I didn't come here to ask for money" (I said).

"If you want to play again and are no longer a cripple, that's another matter. I know you've been in training and working hard. And I've heard that your knee is much better. Is that true? I've seen this kind of situation before. Ex-players come to see me when they're poor or injured or pot-bellied and still want to kick the ball around a bit to pick up some cash. Maybe your case is different. We'll see. I'll take you to do some medical tests today, and to test your strength. Come in, come in, have a beer with me."

In that day I did lots of different medical tests successfully. Jason seemed happy. It was a great thrill for me, but I was not able to say anything

"Ok." (Jason said) "I'm going to save your skin. You're coming out of the slums again. You'll stay in my home for a while. Go get your clothes, right now. Today you start to take vitamins and to train with a coach I trust. I have a really modern gym right in my home. You'll be playing soon enough. We'll decide where – in what country, and with what club. I want to see you scoring goals again."

Unlike many football agents, who are fair-weather friends only interested in athletes with huge paychecks and lucrative contracts and vanish when times are bad, Jason decided to help me. I told him in detail how much I wanted to play again.

I lost no time. In a few hours I was installed in a luxurious room with lots of windows and a magnificent view of the city. That was where my one-of-a-kind agent was in the habit of hiding the players he represented when they were holding out for a better contract or insisting on a transfer. Until the clubs gave in, the players would not show up for the team training sessions. They would just wait there in hiding. It was a simple and effective kind of pressure.

The room was designed to meet the standards of its guests. Tiger-skin rugs, marble walls, pictures of overflowing stadiums and money floating in the air, a garish comforter on the bed, and a television six feet long with great speakers. There was also an elevator to take you to the floor below, where Jason had built a fantastic gym.

My stay at Jason's was a great lesson in living. I would never have thought he was such an unusual person. He lived like an ancient monarch. He had a Jacuzzi in the middle of his dining room. Every day before dinner he would put on flannel pants with a checkered pattern and smoke his pipe. He was nearly seven feet tall, a giant, so to get his body into the water he had to hang his legs over the side.

My unusual agent would put out his pipe, turn on double faucets and with a smile begin his bath ritual. He would start by sprinkling himself with water. Then he would wet his hair with his hand, lather up and invariably complain about something which always bothered him. His toes were revolting. The little toes curled over on top of the others. But all was not lost (so he thought) when he looked at the fine hair on his fat legs.

When he got out of the bathtub, with a towel on his shoulders and his shorts dripping, he would go over to Alina, and brushing hair from her forehead would kiss her tenderly. Moved by these shows of affection, she would embrace him and they would murmur vows of eternal love and fidelity.

Alina always wore pink skirts and pointed shoes. Her behavior was impeccable and she had an easy smile. Her front teeth were constantly on display, like those of a beaver. She was all tenderness and innocence.

I lived with this friendly couple long enough to be able to say that, even though their ideas and upbringing were different (he rather more crude, she somewhat more refined), they understood and respected each other. When they argued, their ill humor only lasted a few minutes. It was moving to see them embracing so often, forgiving each other when the need arose.

One day, at the end of the afternoon, Jason came home in an effusive mood.

"I got you a contract, Daniel! For the next two years you will play in Saudi Arabia. We leave the day after tomorrow. We'll fly first class – I never go in second class. Dixi."

"That's great!" (I said). "That's fantastic! And there's no chance of a hitch?"

"Trust me. In the world of football, there is one method that never fails: cash on the table. Briefcases stuffed with bills. I've known the manager for a long time, so I know who I'm dealing with. When I say yes, it means yes."

"Football is a strange world. Everything revolves around money."

"Not as much as it should" (answered Jason). "Lots of factors have made football a less certain source of wealth. The main reason was TV. In my day the referees could keep a game going for an extra half hour if necessary, until the better team won. I miss those days."

"But that was cheating!" I said.

"No, it wasn't cheating. Nobody was tricking anybody. It was democratic: equal chances for all. Anyone could try to buy the referee, no matter what the color of his skin, or his race or religion. Lots of times I saw referees and owners counting out cash before the games. They were happy, radiant, planning out their lives. Now, no. We are living in strange times. People only talk about cops and phone taps."

Strangely, later that same day, at night while we were having dinner, a police inspector rang the doorbell. He belonged to a unit that dealt with tax fraud. Alina went to the door and spoke harshly to the man.

"What do you want?" she asked.

"Good evening, Ma'am. I would like to speak with Mr. Jason Parker. It's an official matter."

"I'll go see if my husband is available, although I doubt it."

Alina closed the door, returned to the table and calmly began to speak. She praised the cinnamon cake she herself had made for desert. The recipe came from an aunt of hers, now deceased. It was simple: seven eggs, 200 grams of sugar, 150 grams of wheat and two spoonfuls of cinnamon. Delicious!

Meanwhile, with a fork in one hand and the remote control for the TV in the other, Jason was amusing himself, apparently relaxed, watching videos about promising young athletes. The videos came from agents around the world.

"This player knows how to handle the ball" (he said). "But he's really slow. What a slug. He has two speeds: slow and slower. That was a good goal of course, but he kicked the ground more than the ball. Look at the hole in the turf. That's enough, I don't need to see more. This guy doesn't interest me. Let's see the next. An Asian player. Ok, he runs as fast as a Greyhound. But what a bungler. He leaves the ball behind. He has to stop and go back to get it. Awful style. Looks like Bruce Lee. This isn't karate, it's football. Let's see another video. I do this all the time. I see hundreds of videos every month. Now this guy's weight is reasonable. He's from Latin America. But there's something wrong. Look, Daniel, how bad the picture is. It must have been filmed three or four years ago. By now he's probably past his prime. Must weigh twenty pounds more. The great Jason Parker doesn't need to go to the airport on a hoax. Once I went there to meet a player who was supposed to run like the wind and I wound up meeting a guy with a fat ass. Five years had passed since the film I saw was made. Ok, that's it for today, no more videos. I hate it when they try to trick me."

It was hot. Outside, the inspector was waiting patiently. I reminded Jason of this. For a few moments he seemed lost in his thoughts. Suddenly he jumped to his feet, ran up the inside stairs, looked out the window, and watched the officer bite his lips in anger. When the inspector, after so long a wait, turned to go, someone on the second floor threw a large plastic bag full of water on his head.

The next day, the unfortunate officer, now full of spite, drove by Jason's house in a police car with a colleague all morning long, determined to catch him or even to arrest him. They surely thought about Jason's strange character. How was it that such a person, who showed such disrespect for authority, had never been arrested? Where had he laid his extraordinary plans for tax evasion? Where had be bought that enormous plastic water bag?

At a certain point the infernal noise of a motorbike without a muffler interrupted the thoughts of the two policemen. A pizza-delivery boy had parked next to them.

"Good afternoon, gentlemen. Here are your two pizzas."

"Excuse me, we didn't order anything. There must be some mistake." (said the inspector)

"The place I work for told me to bring this order to this place, where there was a police car with this license plate, waiting for these two delicious pizzas. They're already paid for."

"Ok, in that case, hand 'em over. And get that muffler fixed. Your motorbike, the way it is now, is against the law."

The delivery boy got back on his motorbike and took off with a roar, leaving the policemen delighted with their large and unexpected meal. They were vegetarian pizzas with homemade tomato sauce, mayonnaise, eggplant, olives, onion and oregano.

The motorbike could still be heard in the distance when a large motorcycle parked next to the police car. The rider then smashed the window of the police car twice with his right fist. The inspector, with his mouth full, lowered the window and looked out. A big surprise awaited him. There in front of him, with a helmet on his head, Jason was laughing out loud.

"Ha, ha, ha! I hope you're enjoying those pizzas. They were expensive!"

Apparently in a good mood, Jason rose off on his motorcycle, seemingly to go for a ride in the fresh air. The inspector, who the day before had been drenched to the bone by a water bag, was not inclined to mercy. Fuming with wrath, he tried the ignition, ready to go after the offender. The wheels spun around twice, the motor almost ignited. He tried again and this time the motor started up.

The police car, thirty years old and rusting away, with a broken muffler and cracked headlights, was a relic of the earliest days of the automobile, while Jason's bike was the latest Honda model, full of power. The car charged off in a fury and reached a respectable speed for such an old vehicle.

The inspector took a right-hand curve too quickly, fumbling with his hands, which kept crossing over one another on the wheel, and momentarily lost control of the car, which skidded and smashed against a wall. The impact resounded with the crunch of metal and the shattering of glass.

The next day the veteran football player Daniel Malka and the famous agent Jason Parker caught a plan to Saudi Arabia. It was the beginning of a great - and, for me, decisive - adventure.

A few hours after the plane took off under a scalding sun, Jason seemed afraid, lost in thought, summing up his life. He surely didn't want to spend the next few years in jail, thrown in with every kind of rascal. After all, he had money. He could live abroad for a while, telling his lawyers how to torpedo the case against him with absurd filings and appeals.

He began to speak about it.

"I, Jason, Jason Parker of the Parker family, do hereby confess. I had a horrible dream last night, a dream that threw me off balance. I dreamt that I was sleeping in my home and that there outside in the street, in a thick mist, a mysterious figure arose, mounted on a large black stallion. The horseman, tall and athletic, with a sinister air about him, wore a black overcoat and a broad hat, also black. He was a police detective with reeking breath. In a low voice he said my name, "Jason, Jason, Jason," glancing all about with shifty eyes. He seemed to come from far away, judging from the way he spurred his weary steed. The word "murderer" was written all over his restless figure. All living things fled before him, except some evil vultures that fluttered from one rooftop to another, following him wherever he went. His enigmatic air, protruding cheekbones, and the sawed off shotgun he carried in full view all betrayed the secret of his true vocation: contract killer. Suddenly the horse stops in front of my home. The evil detective knows I am sleeping like an angel. But he in incapable of compassion. He wants to arrest me, to kill me. The horse breaks down the door with his front hooves, yet there is no sound. Slowly the animal begins to climb the stairs to my room. Alina is snoring – as she always does when she sleeps on her back. I am in the clouds, deep asleep. I don't hear the steed pacing towards me, his snorting falls on deaf ears. He is a monstrous animal, sweating and famished. He enters the room and eats the first thing he sees: my coat. Then he swallows my tobacco pouch and Alina's purse. The detective bends over me, pulling back the reins. He grabs me by the collar. I am hanging in the air. I wake up in terror. I call out Alina's name. She doesn't hear me. She keeps on snoring. The horse turns around, gallops down the stairs and out of the house, trampling the door he had already smashed down. And away he goes. I am under arrest. The detective's iron grip keeps me suspended in the air. I am crushed by a sense of powerlessness. I know that nothing can save me from paying for my crimes. I weep with remorse. I weep for having played tricks on the police. But it's too late. In the streets of the town beggars and vagabonds who wander through the night look at me with scorn or solidarity. The tireless horse trots on. I see the prison in the distance. It seems like Count Dracula's castle. An iron gate creaks open. I see ovens inside, lots of ovens. Prisoners, naked to the waist, shadowy creatures with scarred faces, are burning tons of garbage in vast ovens. I am dumped next to one of them like a trash bag. I am lost. It was in this terrifying scene that... I regained consciousness. I'll tell you, Daniel, that I decided to flee the country and stay away for a while. I am going with you to Arabia. Alina will join us there."

After listening attentively to Jason's amazing tale, I felt full of vigor and, recalling what Baba Madri had taught me, I said to him in a loud voice:

"So you think you're a prophet, Jason?"

"No" (he answered).

"So then don't attach any importance to your ridiculous dreams. They only reflect your thoughts and anxieties. What you think of during the day is what you dream about at night."

Jason looked at me askance, wondering at my strange wisdom. Where could an ignorant person like me have found such a clear and resounding answer? That must have been what he was thinking. I didn't tell him. Far above the clouds, the airplane continued on its way at 700 miles per hour.

Night fell heavily over the main airport of Saudi Arabia when the Boeing that was carrying us landed with a thud. On the runway airplanes were landing and taking off. A police motorcycle escort approached, followed by four luxury sedans that stopped at the stairs leading down from our plane. Out stepped a group of people whose task was evidently to welcome us.

Together with Jason, I was effusively greeted and welcomed, right under the wing of the aircraft, by representatives of the local prince, who was the club's financial backer and son of the regional sheikh. The men wore white tunics and spoke an Arabic dialect interspersed with improvised phrases in English. We were immediately taken to a luxury beach house with a private boat and a pool, where we would stay and relax from that day on.

I confess that I was quite surprised by everything I found in that most unusual country. I had thought there was nothing there except sand, men praying and women with burqas covering their entire body. But there was much more: lovely modern cities; limousines on brand new avenues with several lanes in each direction; marvelous skyscrapers whose windows gleamed and glistened every day.

The shopping centers were like spaceships, replete with escalators and limpid lakes, with high fashion shops, musical shows in the middle of radiant fountains, museums, movie theaters, restaurants, artificial spots of green all around, and everywhere fresh and smooth-running air conditioning.

The foreign Western population was larger than the native one and seemed strangely adapted to the country and its local laws. There nobody called out for freedom. Rules were to be kept. Any excesses were quickly repressed by rigorous and ubiquitous police and judges. Anyone walking the streets drunk went directly to jail. Unmarried couples could not sleep together. If caught in flagrante they would be imprisoned. There were no prostitutes, no garbage in the streets. Nobody dared to drop a dirty piece of paper or a cigarette butt on the sidewalk. The punishment of thieves was so brutal that no-one dared to touch another's property. The entire society was scandalized by any theft. And if there was any violation of sharia law the authorities immediately ordered a manhunt to track down the offender.

There was a football stadium, with practice grounds and a medical center. There I again became a professional player, though it took real effort. I couldn't squander the opportunity. I knew that there would not be another.

After the training sessions, when my teammates had left, I would stay for an hour to practice passing and heading and to improve ways of controlling the football. I worked hard at passing the ball at the first touch since the shorter the time I had it the less chance there was of being injured by my opponents.

My teammates played with determination, but in front of the goal they had no knack for finishing. They just weren't up to it. They were distracted by the crowd behind the goal. But they were certainly spiritual. Every day, at certain times, they would pray. They would kneel on the ground in submission to God.

One day a reporter had the nerve to say on TV that he had to take tranquilizers before doing his commentary because our team played so badly. And he added:

"This team's fans have to be ready for a lifetime of devotion, since they must be prepared to accept so many losses."

The fans began to hate the reporter. One day, when he came to the stadium to do his commentary during the broadcast of a game, as soon as he stuck his face out of the press box, before his whole head was even visible, he was loudly booed by a chorus of thousands. The booing and hissing were so intense that he declined to proceed with the commentary.

About a hundred fans refused to accept his presence in the stadium, invaded the press box, and began to chase after him as he fled. He ran as fast as he could, with shouts of "Kill him, kill him!" ringing in his ears. He was soon seen escaping from the grounds, racing on foot towards the highway.

That loud-mouthed reporter was lucky to escape unharmed from the attack of fans ready to devour his flesh like wild animals. In the end it was the fans themselves who suffered harm, arrested by the police for their misbehavior. All of them were sentenced that very day to fifty lashes on their bare backs.

The club also had its dictators. The owners paid the players and technical staff well, but took no responsibility for anything that went wrong. It was revolting to see how often, after a defeat, they refused to share any part of the blame. They preferred to place the blame on the coach and players, demanding that they blame themselves during the press conferences, conveniently covering up the lack of oversight and organization that lay behind the losses.

Meanwhile, the worst dictator was the official whose duty it was to keep the turf in good condition. His name was Hassan. Nobody envied him his job, but he had complete control over the grass. Usually the team worked out on artificial turf, but sometimes we needed to practice in the stadium, so the owners would give instructions to prepare the field.

Hassan would go crazy whenever a player kicked the turf and the ball at the same time. He only allowed the field to be used during pre-established practice times, and not for a minute more. As soon as the coach blew the whistle at the end of a training session, Hassan would run onto the pitch like a madman, turn on the sprinkler system and rudely order everyone off the field. Once he tackled me to make sure that the field was free of all players, trainers and balls as soon as possible.

There was one other foreign player on team, besides me. His name was Huang Ke Jinyu. He was a Chinese player, very fast with fine technique. What I remember about him is not just his skill at the game but the childish way he let himself be fooled by an unscrupulous lawyer, also from abroad. Nothing odd about that. Nor was it anything out of the ordinary to see young football players taken in by the facile talk of less than reputable girls who amble around the stadiums trying to attract their attention. Witness me, who married the terrible Renata!

Huang Ke Jinyu listened to nobody, just to his own heart. The result was catastrophic. When his career ended and he checked his bank accounts, there was nothing in any of them. His tricky girlfriend had sacked his wealth and fled to an unknown destination. And what was most dramatic was that Mike had been taking care of nine brothers and sisters and fourteen nieces and nephews, all poor, sick and in constant need of his help. Now he could help nobody. He himself was reduced to want and hunger.

I think the sweltering Arabian sun was bad for my brain. One day, while swimming in the sea, I tried to get back to the shore and realized that the currents not only kept me from making any progress but were steadily sweeping me back out to sea. My heartbeat shot up. Faced with imminent death by drowning I was desperate. My life, so full of dangers, misery, success and failure, of so many sacrifices, seemed about to end in a dreamy sea.

Out of nowhere appeared a sailboat with one man aboard. He calmly asked me:

"Hi, want me to take you back to the beach?"

Helplessly gulping seawater, I cried out, "Yes, yes!" and climbed aboard the miraculous boat, clinging with all my might, with the sense of tragedy that a shipwrecked man might feel on finding a floating piece of wood.

A few minutes later I was kneeling breathless on the beach, next to Jason, who had fallen asleep.

"Jason, Jason, I almost drowned. That sailboat saved my life!"

Jason woke up, still in a daze, and merely said:

"What sailboat?"

I looked out and didn't see any sailboat on the horizon. Jason shut his eyes and fell back into slumber.

It was nearly time for me to leave this lovely country forever glittering in the magnificent sun. I sprinted for the last time around the football field. It was a charming country with its own rituals, customs, unusual laws and courts, and parties in the palace of the local prince.

In my football experience in Arabia I never reached the level of playing that had made me famous in earlier times. The team as a whole did not reach the goals it set for itself. But personally I can't complain. I tried as hard as I could and was useful to the team, although my daily life was marked by many anxieties. Every game or training session that ended without pain in my knees was a joy to me. When the pain returned it meant extreme anguish.

At the end of the second season stipulated in the contract, moved and teary-eyed, I made a painful announcement to my teammates. They were all taken by surprise as I revealed that my professional career was over. I had put my old and weary cleats into a bag, there to remain forever. It was a solemn moment, but nobody paid much attention to what I said. It was time for prayers. My long stint as a player had ended. It was all over.

Aluxury car parked with pomp and circumstance at the main entrance to the airport. Carrying our luggage and bags on our backs Jason and I were on our way home. At a great distance, and with the help of top-notch attorneys, he had won the case that had threatened to deprive him of his freedom, so there was no longer any danger in returning. Alina had left a week before, as if to prepare the way.

"Here we go", said Jason, full of energy. "You can hang up your shoes right now. No more contracts for you, not even I would arrange one. Only on the old-timers team. Ha, ha! It was a nice vacation here. Now it's over. And it's a good thing. This place is too dull and regulated. I like complications. I'm eager to get entangled in the great mass of confusion in our beloved country."

I nodded approval. I was also anxious to get back – to my parents.

"So what is going to happen with your life, Daniel", Jason asked.

"I don't know what's going to happen", I answered. "I only know what's not going to happen. I am going to live alone and am not going to repeat the mistakes of the past. Nobody's going to see me surrounded by parasitic women or showing off fancy cars lined up in a row in my garage, all worth their weight in gold. That would be enough to get poor again in no time at all."

"It's true", Jason said. "Money has a life of its own

and moves and breathes like men. It comes and goes and reproduces. If you don't use money wisely it disappears quickly, no matter how much you have."

At this point Jason paused as though he were suppressing something that he wanted to tell me. He stroked his bushy moustache and launched brusquely into the matter.

"How would you like to be my scout?" he asked.

"Well (I replied) I want to study. In my free time I can look for young talents. I grew up on the street. I know if an athlete is worth his salt or not. If I find some good ones it's only fair that we both earn something from it."

"Ok, excellent", he said. "Creating wealth is hard; sharing it is easier."

The airplane had already taken off a while before. It seemed to be floating on air. No sound could be heard. There was no vibration. I fell asleep and slept for hours. I dreamt of my past: Renata and her family, who had destroyed my wealth with a series of ill thought out and catastrophic business deals.

At 4:33 pm we reached the airport. There was a slight breeze blowing from the east. Everything was calm in the control tower. Ours was just one more airplane. The landing was so smooth that the passengers aboard didn't even notice it. The time of winged jalopies that risked disaster on every flight was long past.

Alina was waiting for us, holding an enormous banner declaring "Welcome!" It was not just for us. Some of Jason's cousins were arriving on another flight. In Africa they had made a fortune in renovations and were now coming to visit their most famous relative. At this point I took my leave.

"Jason, Alina, we'll talk in the next few days. I have to go now. See you soon, pals. I'm forever grateful to you. I feel like a whole man again, thank God!"

"Thank God and Jason Parker, of the Parker family", Jason concluded, while he got ready to greet his cousins.

As a taxi drove me into the city I was struck by an intense yearning to be back in my own country. Shops all open. Traffic lights every fifty yards. Heavy traffic, cars and motorcycles. Throngs of men and women striding along the sidewalks. Children shouting in the street. Cats sitting on window sills. Police. Street-vendors. Newspaper boys. Bustle. Movement. There was not a quiet place for miles around. What a difference from Arabia!

Inside the cab there was a strong smell of food, mixed with the driver's body odor. It seemed unreal. The driver was a woman. She had short black hair, was wearing jeans and a leather shirt, black gloves with the finger tips open. She probably had no children. She spent her time riding around the streets and avenues, obeying the traffic signs, parking on sidewalks. I could tell from the bags under her eyes that she didn't get much sleep.

A red light. The taxi stopped in a line of cars. With her elbow out the window the cab driver shifted her body towards me and pointed a finger in my direction.

"You know, your face seems familiar. Don't I know you from somewhere? Wait, I know. You're Daniel, the famous football player who lost all his money, aren't you?"

"Yes", I said, feeling somewhat ashamed.

"You were a star! I still remember a fantastic goal you scored with a bicycle kick. I was there. What a goal! But you were a fool to lose all your money. And you ruined your wife, Renata, too. I'll tell you, she didn't deserve that."

"Well part of that story didn't happen the way you tell it. But anyway, let's change the topic, if you don't mind. So how are things in this wonderful country? I just got back from a trip abroad."

"Things here ain't so hot. Money is scarce. Business is bad. Every month there's less of it. A lot of small businesses are closing down. Only the big companies are doing well."

"Maybe things will get better. Let's hope so. And there's always football."

"Look, here's your hotel", she said. "I hope you have enough money to pay for the ride."

"I do. Here. Keep the change."

I had already reserved a hotel room about a mile from the street where I grew up, but in a more affluent area, with fresh air. With its striking architecture, gorgeous rooms, pool, restaurant and quiet interior gardens, the hotel offered an absolute guarantee of satisfaction to those who stayed there.

The woman at the reception desk, who spoke like a recording machine, recognized me immediately.

"Good afternoon, Mr. Daniel Malka. We are honored to have you here as a guest. You have a reservation beginning today and for the next seven nights. We trust you will be satisfied with our services."

"I see lots of people coming and going", I responded, surprised. "It's a good sign. Our economy needs to grow. Tourism and the hotel business are an important part of our national wealth nowadays, more and more so."

"Our policy is simple", she said. "The beds must be warm and cozy for every guest."

"Excellent. I'll keep my bed warm. Shall I make a payment now?"

"Yes, Mr. Malka. The whole stay needs to be paid for now."

"I don't understand. I'm just checking in and I have to pay for all seven days?"

"I'm just following orders", she said.

"Ok, then. I won't complain. I'll pay the whole bill right now."

A local tabloid had maliciously printed an article saying that my time in Arabia had not gone well and that I had again spent all my money, leaving behind debts all over the place. My reputation as a spendthrift lived on.

I picked up a standard newspaper. I quickly saw that it would not make for good reading. The headlines were shocking: "War Imminent!" "Corruption Scandal!" "Ballerina Murdered!" "Interest Rates Up Again!" "Marilyn Weds Sixth Husband!" "National Team Hungry for Victory!" "80 Year-Old in Accident!" "Gang Wrecks Restaurant!"

My experience in Arabia, after the profound teachings of Baba Madri, had made me a man full of faith and hope. I set the newspaper aside in disgust. The world that the media shows, a world of violence, pornography and destruction, is not the real world. Of course there are marginal areas where the cruelest moral degradation reigns. My own street had all the necessary ingredients. But that is not the world. The world is a gigantic place, with great beauty and even admirable organization.

Considering the concentration of poverty and the exposure of people of all ages to vices during decades on end, I am convinced that even on my street there was never so much violence or immorality as one might expect. Most of the women had never been murderers or whores; the men were not rapists or cold-blooded killers. I myself had never been shot or squashed into the ground. That was where I had spent my youth. And, unexpectedly, that was where I would live again.

It was early morning when I went out onto the street. The first rays of the sun were spreading over the earth. Everything seemed asleep. Only the cats and dogs watched me, curious. Garbage bins had been dumped onto the sidewalk and bloody rags lay in the entryways of buildings. Nothing else could be seen beneath the laundry lines creaking as they swayed back and forth with clothes hung out to dry.

As I walked in front of Baba Madri's house, the door suddenly swung open revealing a richly dressed figure.

"I was waiting for you", said Madri, with suitcase in hand.

"How happy I am to see you", I said. "I just arrived. What's with the suitcase? Are you off on a trip?"

"I am leaving today for the land where my fathers died. I haven't been back there since I was a child."

"What time is your flight?" I asked.

"I'm going on foot. It makes me feel happy to stretch my legs. I'll try to keep walking, night and day. If I have to stop late at night, I'll be back on the trail by dawn. I have no intention of coming back here."

"You are walking? Wait a minute. Aren't you a bit old for that?"

"Silence!" he said.

Baba Madri put his right arm around my neck, as a father would do to his son, and led me inside the house.

"I have often dreamed of this day", I said. "I was not just hoping to see you off. I want to tell you how good these last two years have been for me. God gave me the strength to play football again. I made a lot of money. This time I didn't get dazzled by excesses and absurd investments. I saved what I earned. I have much more than I need, because from now on I am going to live a simple and frugal life. I won't be showing off my wealth. I'm not going to buy a car. And this time I'm going to avoid bad company. Now I feel that I have grown up. I am going to help my parents. I'm going to study. I'll spend some time trying to recruit talented young football players. But other than that I want to study, I want to learn, I want to get some real culture. I am really ignorant. There is so much that I have never read, never learned, and time is passing. Now I am going to devote myself to those things."

"And after that?" Baba Madri asked.

"Well, after the next couple of years, I don't know. I suppose my studies will make me want to learn more. So I will probably keep on studying and reading more and more as the years go by."

"And after that?" he asked again.

"Well, I think that's the only answer I can give. As the years go by -- maybe four, six, eight, fifteen years -- I will want to learn and study even more."

"And after that?"

"After that I will be old! What else do I need to know?" I asked, unable to stop the questions and answers that were brimming on my lips.

"There is a kind of heroism that passes unnoticed. Nobody sees it. It consists of doing the right thing every day. Happiness corresponds to a peaceful state of mind. To be at peace with God, with the cosmos, with men. To achieve that you have to affect the lives of many other people. The worth of a man's life is measured by how many lives he touches."

"How can I touch the lives of many others? By giving money to the poor? That's impossible. There are millions of poor people. I don't have enough money to help them all."

"Material wealth belongs to God", Madri said calmly. "You should ask yourself what God wants you to do with the wealth he has entrusted to you."

"I don't understand", I said. "I saved up money for two years. I made a lot of sacrifices. Isn't that money mine? I don't get it. I don't think I'll ever understand that way of thinking."

"What is there that doesn't change? Rocks?"

"What can God want me to do with my wealth", I asked, with a sinking feeling.

"We have already talked about the special mission that every soul has. I will help you to discover what your mission is, so long as you promise me that you will fight against your lower instincts. To use their own free will God gave men yetzer tov (the inclination to good) and yetzer hará (the inclination to evil). The special mission of each soul is completely undermined by yetzer hará."

"What is the specific mission of my soul?" I asked.

"The answer is more difficult than the question", said Madri. "I will tell you a little story".

"I love stories", I said. "Please begin. I'll be glad to listen."

"Many years ago, in a far-away land (Madri said, beginning his narrative), there was a community that lived well beneath the poverty level. The situation was frightening: cold, hunger, suffering, lack of work, no social structures to provide for health and justice. The State did nothing there except keep the people down-trodden and collect taxes. The infants cried and moaned night after night, day after day. Old men met premature deaths. They died inconsolable, leaving their offspring a future fraught with fear. Everybody lacked joy, food and healthcare. There was nothing to counteract this unbelievable poverty except one man, who was very wealthy, since God had blessed him with a large fortune. He had enough gold to help many people. If he wanted to. But he didn't want to. He helped nobody. He was avaricious. He himself lived on next to nothing. He had no wife, no children, and lived without conveniences or entertainment."

"What a loathsome man", I said, feeling anger.

"One day, the father of a large family came to the home of this avaricious man. He had eight children and no job. His wife was ill. His children were doomed to a life of famine. This unlucky man felt humiliated to sit there telling the story of his misfortune. There was not even electricity in his home. He wept and wept. The miser listened to him attentively. The man's story seemed to inspire compassion in him. But when the visitor asked him for some money his mood changed completely. He became angry. Instead of compassion he felt rage. He began to yell. To his mind nobody had the right to go to his house and ask him for money. So he told the poor man to leave."

"The whole life of the miser consisted of hoarding money and disdaining others", I said.

"Not long after, another poor man, who looked like a vagabond, ran into the miser in the street, fell to his knees and began to cry. He was 90 years old. He had no strength left to struggle. His son had severe mental problems and was confined to bed. The man was crying out in pain. His body was covered with sores, and he had eaten nothing for days. He was cold, he needed clothes. Maybe some money could alleviate the tragedy. But the miser was insensitive to the suffering of others. He reprimanded the old man and sent him packing. Throughout his life this miser was approached by many people in need of help, who looked to him as their last hope. All of them told him sad and moving stories of their suffering. But nothing moved him enough to help them. His heart was hard, he helped nobody, gave nobody any money, not even food, water, clothing or medicine."

"The whole community must surely have been hated this man", I said, taking a deep breath.

"Everyone called him a miser (Baba Madri continued). Nobody greeted him kindly. Children threw stones at him. Some people spat at him, others struck him. He finally withdrew to his house, only venturing out once a week late at night. And so it went for years, for decades. A long time later the miser had to leave his home and go far away. Nobody missed him. He had long lived in utter solitude. His house seemed permanently closed. But the miser was much more important to the community than people thought."

"And why was that?" I asked, amazed. "It's hard to imagine anybody who could be of less use to the people around him."

"A few days after the miser disappeared, a woman sat down on the landing of a stairwell in her building and began to scream in utter despair, saying someone had robbed her. She and her invalid husband and teenage children were hungry. People asked her what had been stolen. She said she that for a long time she had gotten an envelope from an anonymous source and that the money which it contained was what kept her family going. This time the envelope had not appeared. The poor woman's cries of grief were still echoing when another woman, who was walking along the street, began to tell a similar tale. She too was used to finding an envelope under her door with some money in it, not much, but still enough to be useful in raising her children. The envelope, she said, usually was together with children's books. The news crackled around the neighborhood like gunpowder. More screams. More women. And men too. All of them had the same story to tell. Poor but honorable families, they expressed their sense of desolation, their sadness and consternation. The man who had left, the man they loathed, thinking him a miser, had during decades been the unknown pillar of their happiness."

After listening closely to every detail of Baba Madri's extraordinary tale, which moved and inspired me, I felt full of energy and good will, and interrupted him to exclaim:

"My God! I love that story. How amazing!"

"Now you draw the consequences", responded Madri. "Those who possess wealth should distribute wisely what they can spare: money and books full of life and energy. Food brings nourishment, medicine can cure illness, clothes provide warmth, and education sets men free."

"I already told you: I don't have that much money", I said. "How many families in the world are in need? Millions!"

Proving more and more the strength of his will, Baba Madri calmly continued his discourse.

"God doubles the wealth of those who give anonymously. There are eight levels of charity, and the third highest is when the person who receives does not know who the giver is. It is important that the identity of the giver be unknown. But it's not easy to keep the secret. One has to maintain silence. An old proverb says that it takes two years to learn to talk and sixty to learn to keep one's mouth shut. Every friend has a friend, and that friend has a friend, and so on."

"I'm sorry to say (I said) that I really don't have enough money to..."

"Stop!" he said. "Don't make me waste my time in useless talk. I must leave now. From now on my home belongs to you."

"What home? I don't want to live in this house."

"Done", he said.

"I want to live far away from this street", I said. "I spent my childhood and adolescence here. There's not enough to eat, the place is run by gangs, everybody is fighting with everybody else about everything. I grew up to the sound of old men crying, where the rooms were stuffed with people shivering from the cold, where families were kicked out of their apartments, where beggars were doubled over in pain. Never again!"

"I have been living here for almost a century", replied Baba Madri calmly. "I know the story inside and out. You are going to live in my home. I won't take no for an answer. The legal documents have already been taken care of. I wish you well. Maybe we will meet in another time. Best of luck!"

That day, my mind full of questions, I walked with Baba Madri as far as I could. It was impossible to talk him out of the idea of giving me his home. And I could not get him to answer my questions about the special mission assigned to my soul. This unique old man was entirely focused on his journey. Over and over he said that he meant to keep on walking, no matter how hard the trip.

I remember seeing him carrying his suitcase, facing into the wind, walking quickly down a hill covered with green grass. It seemed that his breathing, though strangely transformed by the distance, could still be heard. And so Madri strode off into the distance towards his destiny, with dignity -- as always. Alone.

The next day I put on ordinary clothes, assumed an air of simplicity, and moved into Baba Madri's home. The neighbors were all puzzled when they saw me going in and out of that enigmatic dwelling. Still, Madri inspired such awe that nobody dared to ask me any questions. Even the gang members and drug dealers on the street diverted their gaze as they walked by me.

With Madri's departure the path of my soul began to be inscribed without my even knowing it. A few days after I moved into his house, even before the electricity had been turned on, significant events began to occur. Esther, my friend since childhood, saw me in the street and ran towards me, crying.

"Daniel, Daniel, help me, please! I need some money. I beg you. I have nothing to eat, no food for my children. We are all cold and hungry. I always promised myself that one day they would have the things I never had. But it hasn't happened. They have even less than I did."

"What has happened, Esther?" I asked. "Did you lose your job? I never imagined you begging for anything."

"Oh Daniel (she said), I haven't had a job for ten years. I only had one job and I lost it long ago. My marriage didn't work out either. Life is really tough. I feel so defeated. I've even thought of stealing just to survive."

"But Esther, how have you survived during all these years? How have you managed to feed and clothe your children?"

"Every week for years someone slipped an envelope with money in it under the door of my apartment. It wasn't much, but it was a big help. And often there were books for children there too. This week there was no envelope, no money, no books. I feel desperate", said Esther, while she folded and unfolded the last envelope she had received.

That same day I saw a blind woman seated on the sidewalk, crying convulsively. She was in danger of losing her apartment because she couldn't pay the rent. She looked famished and miserable. She didn't know what to do. She spoke openly of suicide and said she had been robbed. I leaned over and asked her who had robbed her. She told me about an envelope with money that had always appeared under the door of her apartment.

Later an old man looking like a corpse banged on the door of my parents' home. They knew him well. He had been in ill health and poor all his life and had been a victim of discrimination. Nobody cared about him. Now, well into his sixties, his life was devoid of any joy or hope or human dignity.

He sat down at the table and poured his heart out. He couldn't keep from crying. Tears drenched his cheeks. I was moved and troubled to hear him bemoan his fate. For many years he had depended on some money that appeared mysteriously underneath his door every week. This time there was nothing.

In the next few hours I realized there were other cases, all similar. The poor but honorable families on the street were all tremendously upset. They were no longer receiving the mysterious and anonymous weekly gift of money that had allowed them to pay for basic necessities.

I soon realized who was behind those gifts. He had left to return to his own country only a few days before. Now he was already far away. Maybe he had reached his destination. I imagined him walking along with a sense that he had fulfilled his duty.

Instead of spending his life – like most rich men — basking on a sunny beach or watching TV, as if hunger and extreme suffering did not exist, or simply criticizing the lack of any public policy to fight poverty, Baba Madri had donated a large part of his time and financial resources to families that lived below the poverty level, without human dignity. He had done it anonymously, in silent solidarity with the poor. And he had done it with great wisdom. Any small amount that can regularly be added to the minimal resources of needy families is like an enormous treasure.

Some years have passed since Baba Madri left. His huge library has been my faithful companion during all this time. In the street, the people nearly reduced to animals by the struggle for their daily bread, or physically weakened, don't even suspect that this great sea of books exists, so rich in the teachings of God and history.

Now I have read many books, but there are still many more left to read. Every day I wonder whether the writers who worked so hard to produce them wound up losing or gaining from their labor. It is an honor for me to be keeper of this treasure. And it was a great stroke of good fortune. I am no longer half a man.

What money I have I give anonymously to families on this street of mine. I continue to be Madri's secret replacement in the home that was his, trying to get my heart and mind to rise to the occasion and take on so great a responsibility. "What did you do for society today?" he asked me once. I don't feel old or tired of pulling my oar. I know that ancient sage's secret of longevity and also the secret of his inner peace.

THE END

Thank you for reading.

We invite you to share your thoughts and reactions.

Subscribe

<u>JohnRoseAuthor.com</u>

WHAT A FOOTBALLER!

Author: John Rose
© John Rose
Graphic Project: Evolua Edições
Design: Frederica Claro de Armada

1st edition: 2022

Largo do Mosteiro, 120, Lj17
4435-346 Rio Tinto
geral@edicoes.evolua.pt
964075601 / 969614994